Terror Tree's Pun Book of Horror Stories

Edited by
Stephanie Ellis & S.G. Mulholland

Terror Tree's Pun Book of Horror Stories © 2015
KnightWatch Press

DIYary of the Dead © James Brogden
Trees Behind You © Lisamarie Lamb
Logan's Runs © Nick Walters
Blood on Santa's Claw © Richard Freeman
Road Rage © David Croser
The Thin Dead Line © O.L. Humphreys
Dead Punny © Ross Baxter
The Woman in Slacks © Stephanie Ellis
Tie Bride © T.M. McLean
The Round of the Baskervilles © Jon Charles
Rosemary's Baby Shower © Ken MacGregor
Twi-tard © Scott Harper
Cycle Killer © Nick Walters
Poo the Winged Serpent © Richard Freeman
A Stitch in Frankenstein Saves Nine © Stewart Hotston
Spyder, Spyder © David Croser
Olé Bubba and the Forty Steves © James Dorr
The Dreams that Stuff is Made Of © William Meikle

Cover artwork © 2015 Bob Veon

Cover design © 2015 Great British Horror

All rights reserved.

Published in Great Britain in 2015 by
KnightWatch Press
Birmingham, UK

CONTENTS

DIYary of the Dead	James Brogden	1
Trees Behind You	Lisamarie Lamb	7
Logan's Runs	Nick Walters	13
Blood on Santa's Claw	Richard Freeman	25
Road Rage	David Croser	37
The Thin Dead Line	O.L. Humphreys	47
Dead Punny	Ross Baxter	65
The Woman in Slacks	Stephanie Ellis	75
Tie Bride	T.M. McLean	91
The Round of the Baskervilles	Jon Charles	103
Rosemary's Baby Shower	Ken MacGregor	109
Twi-tard	Scott Harper	117
Cycle Killer	Nick Walters	123
Poo the Winged Serpent	Richard Freeman	137
A Stitch in Frankenstein Saves Nine	Stewart Hotston	147
Spyder, Spyder	David Croser	163
Olé Bubba and the Forty Steves	James Dorr	177
The Dreams that Stuff is Made Of	William Meikle	189

DIYary of the Dead
by James Brogden

George Dewey stepped back from the wall in the upstairs hallway to assess his handiwork. The new wallpaper strip hung straight and clean, with the floral pattern matching exactly along each edge. Louise had made it clear how much she hated the design, but that hardly mattered now. She wasn't currently in a position to either hate or love anything. He squinted at it from several angles, looking for tell-tale shadows where the light caught …

Ah. There. Low down, just above the skirting board and approximately the size of a fifty pence piece.

A bubble.

Sometimes, with the best will in the world and no matter how methodical one was – and George prided himself on being a particularly methodical man – tiny air bubbles will collect under a sheet of freshly hung wallpaper and collect as blisters like this. It didn't bother him over-much; he knew how to deal with it.

Taking a damp sponge, he firmly but carefully smoothed it out, working towards the edge of the sheet, leaving it nice and flat again.

Then, with a tiny, almost inaudible little *fup!* sound, it reappeared. It was closer to the near-invisible line where this sheet joined its neighbour, and slightly smaller, but definitely there.

He pushed his glasses higher on his nose and frowned at the offending blister.

This should not have happened. The paper was heavy gauge, cloth-backed vinyl – the most expensive that B&Q could offer. He was an experienced paper-hanger; he'd redecorated their – sorry, his, he reminded himself – house every five years from top to bottom. This shouldn't have happened.

He took the sponge and smoothed it out again.

There was another little *fup!* As the blister popped up again.

This time it was on the other side of the join, which was physically impossible. The air in the bubble should have escaped when it reached the edge, but there it was. Staring at him.

Clearly this was going to take something a bit more drastic. He rummaged in his tool box for a Stanley knife, and frowned again when he couldn't find it. This too was most unusual – he was always so meticulous about looking after his tools. It was one of the many things which Louise, apparently, hadn't been able to stand about him. Well, that had gone both ways, hadn't it? He'd always hated her untidiness, though he'd never been such a nag as to keep on at her about it. Take the way her feet were sticking out of the bedroom doorway down the hall now, one shoe hanging off. Typical.

Then he remembered where the Stanley knife was. He went into the bedroom and saw it lying next to her.

"There you are, you little so-and-so," he chided.

He took it through to the en-suite – added when the boys had grown too big for all of them to share the family bathroom comfortably – and carefully washed off all the blood. It was important to keep one's tools in good condition, after all.

"Meticulous," he said to her as he passed back through the bedroom. "From the Latin 'metus', meaning 'fear'. That's what we call ironic, my darling."

Going back to the impossible blister, he cut a single line precisely down its centre and smoothed each half down while the glue was still tacky. It would leave a barely perceptible scar in the paper when it dried, which was a shame, but he supposed that occasionally sacrifices like that needed to be made.

Louise had never understood the kinds of sacrifices which were necessary to have a well-kept and organised family home – not until the end, anyway.

He was going to have to do something about her clothes, which had sprayed all over the bedroom out of her suitcase when she'd swung it at his head. He didn't have a clue how to fold or where to put things like her bras, but he supposed he could just give them straight to a charity shop since she'd never be wearing them again. Especially the fancy frilly ones that he'd found she'd been buying secretly from Ann Summers, and certainly not wearing for his benefit.

There was a little *fup!* from low down, near the floor.

Directly below where he'd excised the bubble, another one of exactly the same shape and size had appeared in the paint of the skirting board. It might have been mistaken for a different one, but George knew better. And it wasn't just staring at him – it was openly mocking him. Just like she'd mocked him, with her fancy frilly lacy knickers and the other things she'd bought from that filthy shop. She'd waved a big black dildo in his face and yelled "Well why not? It's what I've learned from you, after all, isn't it? Do it your fucking self?" For a moment he wanted to smash and gouge that bubble from the wall with a hammer, a crowbar, his fingernails and teeth ...

He drew a deep breath and forced himself to calm down. One thing at a time. Air blisters in paint required a different technique entirely.

He took the blister away with a paint scraper and sanded back the flaking edges with a sanding block, then primed the new bare patch of wood and went over that with some white gloss once it had dried. It took about two hours. At some point during the process he thought he heard a heavy slithering bump from the bedroom, but couldn't spare any attention from his focus on the job at hand. She'd always complained that he never paid her any attention when he was fixated on one of his 'bloody stupid projects', and he didn't see why that should change just because she was dead.

He made himself a cup of tea and went back upstairs to sit on their bed, surrounded by her lacy underthings and her blood which had jetted up the walls and swamped the carpet in a stinking red-brown flood. Suddenly his heart sank at the awful waste of it all. That carpet had been nearly fifteen quid a square metre; you didn't see that kind of value for money these days.

It vaguely crossed his mind to wonder where Louise had gone, but he had to finish his jobs first. One thing at a time.

As he reached the point where he'd repainted the skirting board, he heard a very familiar but much heavier *flump!* sound and the carpet beneath his bare foot lifted up in a blister as big as a cereal bowl. He actually saw it pop up, almost as if it had been trying to trip him.

"No," he admonished it. "Just …," he waved his mug at it for emphasis. "No! Do you hear me?" Angrily, he stamped on the bubble.

The instant it deflated, his foot was seized by a savage cramp of agony, and a massive blister the size of a golf ball erupted in the skin on the back of it, close to where it joined his ankle. He yelled in fright and fell backwards onto his arse. He grabbed his ankle, and without stopping to really think about what he was doing, pushed down on the blister with both thumbs.

It reappeared higher up, on the side of his calf.

He tried to massage it away, but it just slithered from under his grip and ended up behind his knee. Moaning in panic, he squeezed, kneaded, pummelled and punched his flesh to make the hideous thing gone, but each time he succeeded only in driving it higher and higher until somewhere towards his navel it disappeared. Instead of feeling victorious he knew with a sick certainty that this only meant that it was now inside him, and that his every movement – his every breath – was driving it deeper and deeper.

He froze, completely overwhelmed with terror and at a loss for what to do. This was the most terrifying thing of all: not what was happening to him, but that he, who was usually so capable, had no idea how to fix it himself.

And then Louise was there with the solution. Dear, sweet, loving Louise, who had forgiven him again as she had always forgiven his embarrassing, childish tantrums. She was finding it a little hard to walk, and he thought he must have cut some of the tendons in her legs accidentally, as she shuffle-slipped out of the family bathroom towards him, bumping against the wall and leaving a long smear of blood on his new wallpaper. One hand was demurely trying to hold together the slashed remains of her dress and her stomach, but the damage to her hands meant that they kept slipping open, revealing glimpses of her internal organs like an obscene burlesque act. There was no possibility that she might be alive, nor that she might talk – her throat was far too ruined for either.

All she could do was glare at him with the glittering intensity of her hatred as she handed him the thing in her other hand. The tool he needed to finish the job. The Stanley knife. She wasn't going to spare the effort to kill him, and in the end she didn't even need to speak; the message in the offering was clear enough.

Do it yourself.

"I love you," he whispered in a voice wet with tears of gratitude and terror.

Slowly and clumsily, she finished her own job, which was to leave him.

The blister was still inside him somewhere, so he pressed the blade to his flesh and began to look for it.

edited by Stephanie Ellis & S.G. Mulholland

Trees Behind You
by Lisamarie Lamb

Marcus tapped the top of the pile of greasy, crumbling earth with his shovel and wiped his forehead, managing to smear a thick smudge of soil across it. The dark dirt set itself deep into the lines that had somehow appeared there over the years, gaining purchase each time he looked in the mirror, cutting further into the flesh as each lonely birthday passed, but he hardly noticed. He smiled to himself. Nodded to himself. Felt pleased with himself.

Another job well done.

Another load of trees planted in the old orchard.

Another paycheck on the way. The last one before the big one, if he had planned it right. And he *had* planned it right. He had been working on the scheme for so long, so so many years, that there was nothing that could stop him now. Surely not. Surely nothing.

Marcus swung his shovel up and over his shoulder, letting it fall heavily to rest there, grunting, bearing the brunt of the weight of it. It was a good weight, the sort of weight that meant he'd done some hard work and was going to be rewarded for it. The sort of weight that meant he had earned what he was about to get. Oh yes. Aching arms and creaking knees and all of it.

The saplings he had planted that day swayed in the light breeze, and he waved back at them, winking. Funny little things, so weak and worthless, nothing at all like the trees that they would become. Or rather, would never become. If he had planned wrong (which he knew he hadn't, was *sure* he hadn't), they'd grow up strong, healthy, nourished by the good soil and the clean air. And they would provide enough fruit to make cider or sauce or pies or whatever anyone wanted to do with the stuff. Marcus didn't care. He didn't eat his own fruit. Never would. It was too much like eating money, which had never appealed to him. But if he had planned right, they wouldn't even make it. Cut down in their prime, as the old saying went. And Marcus would be glad of it.

He stepped back to take one more look at the orchard, the entirety of it. It was immense. He hadn't really needed to add the saplings to his horde, but there was a space, just a tiny little block of emptiness, so he felt he should fill it. It was a compulsion for him now, a habit. Anyway, the more the better, surely? It all came down to money in the end.

Money and Marcus' love of the stuff.

Ha. The root of all evil if old myths could be believed, but so what? Money was all that counted these days, and he would enjoy counting his.

It had been a while since Marcus had dug down deep into the orchard's heart, a while since he had visited at all, even though he had dreamed about it and longed to feel the earth – his earth for the moment – as it melted in his hands and clamped itself to his finger. As he stepped away, the older, more established trees rustling in that same slight breeze, he thought he caught sight of something that jumped between trunks and hung in the darkening air. A shadow, or an imagining, flickered across his vision. But Marcus knew that he was the only one in the orchard. He had to be. He was the only one allowed there until harvest time, which was still a month or more away. And this year he was tempted not to hire anyone from the village at all. He would do it himself since it would be the last time, or so he hoped. That, just like the planting of the new saplings, was something to pass the time while he waited for the men in expensive suits to come back.

And yet ... still ... there was something ... more. Something more. Something else.

Marcus' chest tightened and his legs felt loose around the joints, knees like sponge and hips like water. *There was no one, there was no one, there was no one.* But as many times as he repeated this to himself, as many times as he urged himself to believe it, he couldn't quite shake the black shape from his eyes, from his brain. From his soul. It had made the world cold.

Marcus shot his hands beneath his armpits and hugged himself close, wanting to move, to leave this place that had once been full of sunlight but was now achingly chill and deepeningly melancholic, but unable to persuade his leaden feet from their place in the elastic ground.

Had the trees moved?

Marcus, who desperately wanted to run, run, as fast as he could so he would be beyond capture, couldn't even blink for fear of something attacking him. Could have sworn they had. The saplings now seemed to be huddled together, fearful, no longer waving but crying out for help. And the bigger trees, the massive ones Marcus had planted with his grandfather, with his father, with his brother, with his wife, with his children, now loomed above him, closer than they had been, closer by far even though they could not possibly have moved, their roots trapping them in the ground forever.

And ever.

The root of all evil.

No, they hadn't moved. They couldn't have moved.

Marcus breathed in, held the breath, exhaled slowly and surely and felt immediately better for it. It was just the gathering gloom. It was just the setting sun. It was just the realisation that rain was beginning to fall in soft, splattering drops that felt fine and misty and good on Marcus' flushed face. That was all. Nothing had moved. Nothing was coming for him. His heart was not about to explode out of his chest and his bones were not made of rubber.

The man laughed to himself. Foolish, foolish thoughts.

He laughed again, hoping that it would scare away the bad thoughts.

Marcus twisted the handle of his shovel until it felt comfortable in his grip and then saluted the orchard, saying his goodbyes. It wouldn't do to be impolite, even if his good manners were hanging on the very edge of sarcasm. He took one step, two, three steps, four, and on his fifth step, he tripped, his ankle twisted, and he fell to the ground, wailing at the sudden pain. He let go of the shovel and grabbed at his leg, cursing through his teeth. He had a long walk ahead, back down to the farm, and now he would have to hobble, use the shovel as a walking stick. He glanced up at the sky. The rain was coming quicker now, heavier. And the dark was dropping down on the world like an eyelid closing.

Marcus hauled himself to his good foot, hopped feebly, hating his luck. It was almost a pity there was no one left to help him. Almost. No one would see him staggering down the dirt track, back to the house. Maybe that was for the best. A thought tugged at him then, unwelcome and unwanted; he had *chosen* to be alone. He had *made* himself alone. It was his fault if he had to struggle now.

No.

It was only a twisted (hopefully not sprained, hopefully not broken) ankle. Nothing too bad. Nothing to regret anything about.

No.

Marcus cleared his head of such dark and dangerous thoughts. A few moments of pain were worth the gain of having the orchard to himself. Ever since the developers had knocked on his door those few months ago and shown him a cheque – with his, and only his, name on it – for more money that he would ever see through farming, through harvesting and selling his apples, no matter how many extra trees he planted, he had chosen to be alone. He wouldn't share his unexpected windfall.

He certainly had never planned to.

And with a well-worded invitation for his family to join him in the orchard, one at a time, one by one, and with a well-placed blow of his good old shovel, he cleared the path to his fortune.

Was it any wonder, then, that Marcus refused to eat his own fruit, knowing as he did what was feeding the trees on which it grew?

As Marcus shuffled away, going slowly but making progress, he heard the sound again. A muffled crying, a crunching shout. This time he refused to turn around even as the shadows drew nearer. The trees could move. The bodies could scream. He would have his money and if he didn't acknowledge that there was a problem then there wasn't one.

Only there was.

It was creeping ever closer.

Marcus didn't make a sound as his skull broke and scattered across the orchard. The ground barely noticed as he landed in a tangled mess of blood and bone.

The man in the suit smiled as he began to dig Marcus' grave. The orchard was his now, and he'd only had to sell his soul to get it.

edited by Stephanie Ellis & S.G. Mulholland

Logan's Runs
by Nick Walters

It all started when my wife bought the blooming thing back from a car boot sale. Never liked those affairs. Full of shysters and gypos and chavs all trying to offload their junk. Glorified jumble sale if you ask me. Wife loved them, though. Always something interesting to discover, always a bargain or two. Well this time she brought back more than she bargained for. Sorry. Bad taste. Trying to make the best of things. Not good at jokes, never have been.

She thrust the object in question right under my nose as I was making my way through *The Times* after a hearty Sunday lunch, a lunch I'd cooked but which she'd neglected in favour of her beloved 'car booty.'

"Look at this!" she hooted. Something black obscured my vision.

I scrambled out of my chair. "Look at what! Damn rubbish!" I growled.

She thrust it into my hands. Its surface was cool and curved and it was the weight of a substantial desk dictionary. I held it out in front of me the better to examine it.

It was a toilet seat.

A shiny black toilet seat complete with lid.

"Look inside."

Somewhat nonplussed I placed the object down on the dining-room table. The lid glistened like the carapace of some giant insect.

"Go on, open it!"

"Why did you buy this? We've got perfectly decent bog seats as you know! Bloody ridiculous," I rumbled, but knew that for the benefit of a quiet life it was always best to obey Freya. I lifted up the lid. It moved with slight resistance, and stayed propped open at an angle of about seventy degrees.

"Bloody Nora." I was not prepared for the sight that met my eyes. The seat was painted the same jet black as the lid, but it was inscribed with luminescent symbols which looped their way around the seat in a manner which made me feel strangely ill. My guts rumbled as I clocked that a great orange and purple snake was intertwined with the pattern, its mouth open as if to consume its own tail. The more I looked, the more detail I saw: fiendish imps frolicked, naked nymphs cavorted, strange figures seemed to glow with their own inner light. My guts rumbled again. Probably the sprouts.

"Lovely, isn't it? Where's lunch?"

I waved in the general direction of the microwave, unable to look away from the object. I picked it up and turned it over. There on the rear – which was otherwise unmarked – was a small metal plate indented with a manufacturer's mark bearing the name 'CONNINGTON.' The name evoked stout English craftsmanship and the lost values of a golden era long past where you could leave your door open and there was a Bobby on every street. The total opposite of the reckless, sick, bacchanalian weirdness portrayed on the other side. That muck must have been added later. I snorted. Gypos.

I put it back on the table with a clunk and wandered off into the garden, my stomach rumbling again, and this time there was a sharp stabbing pain somewhere inside my (admittedly rather prodigious) abdomen.

After an hour or so bimbling around the garden doing some weeding (bloody bindweed) I went inside again. My house and garden are panacea to my soul. In retirement I can truly enjoy them in a way I never could during my long career in the Civil Service, when there'd always been acres of paperwork to take home, and nights away in London. My house had seemed transparent to me then, as though it only existed around me as I flitted ghost-like through the days without seeing or feeling. Or it had seemed like a pit-stop where I merely refuelled and refreshed, not lived properly. In either case, nothing like a proper home.

Retirement had given my home back to me. Freya still had her career of course – she was ten years younger – and the world will always need fashion journalists. (Another joke. Told you I was bad at them). If it wasn't for all the crap she brought back from car booties I would enjoy the house even more, I thought as I passed through the dining room where the object still lay on the table, lid still raised as if waiting for use. I stepped over and shut the lid. Bloody rubbish. Then I felt a prickling of guilt. Freya was not a bad wife by any means and it had taken me two previous marriages to find someone like her. Should be grateful I suppose. Characteristic of retired male to find stuff to grumble about, I supposed again as I hauled myself up the stairs.

I went into the bathroom and looked down at the toilet seat as if with new eyes. It was a plain affair with a seat of dark oak, and it seemed friendly and welcoming, innocent and pure compared to the monstrosity downstairs. I undid my belt and slid my trousers down. Always sat down to pee, lost that particular battle long ago, anything for a quiet life. More comfy anyway and I could flick through one of the travel books I kept next to the loo.

Comfy. How comfy my life, you must be thinking. Retired Civil Servant, no money woes, house owned outright, sexy (relatively) young wife, kids with good careers. And you're right. I am comfy. What's wrong with that? Have I not earned this life? What do I care what you think anyway. I don't need your or anyone's approval.

Ablutions over, I wandered downstairs again. The offending object was no longer on the kitchen table. Hmm! Freya'd probably tidied it away somewhere. I hoped I'd seen the last of the thing, and sat down in front of the telly for the golf.

***

Bastarding thing turned up again the very next day.

I'd been out meeting old colleagues for the annual reunion lunch, a bitter-sweet affair because there would always be some fresh tragedy. A death, a discovery of disease, a divorce, the usual everyday events that shatter lives. This one hadn't been too bad. Phil's cancer was in remission, and Ian had got back with his wife Karen (though we all doubted it would last), and no-one had died. I drove home in the Volvo relatively light of heart with Vivaldi on the Blaupunkt.

By the time I got home I was in dire need, so I parked the car in the drive without bothering with the fiddly garage door, let myself in (Freya was at work) and trotted with my legs crossed (so to speak) up the stairs. I opened the bathroom door and there it was. Black and shiny like a beetle. A moment of doubt – could I be sure? Perhaps it was just a normal black loo seat. But I knew it wasn't and a quick tilt of the cover to glimpse those evil doodlings was enough to confirm it.

I straightened up, wincing at the pain in my stomach again. Damn that woman! How dare she get rid of my trusty wooden throne and replace it with this misbegotten artifact? I still needed to relieve myself, so I raised the lid fully and – and I could not bring myself to do it. I could not park my posterior on that abomination. I grimaced. The fangs on that snake looked almost real.

I banged the lid down and went back downstairs, through the kitchen and into the back garden. No, I wasn't about to water the nasturtiums; we had an outside khazi. Trap Two. Had it installed back when I was in the Service and we entertained a lot. Saved people traipsing through the house at garden parties and barbecues. Didn't have many parties these days so the outside khazi had become my retreat, my place to hide when Freya and I argued (which didn't happen often, but when it did, believe me, a man needed a place to lie low).

Although it was May there was still a nip in the air and I shivered as I darted across the lawn and slid back the bolt of the wooden shed that housed Trap Two. Inside the smell of pine disinfectant and paint soothed me (I'd given it a lick a few weeks ago, pale blue to make it seem more spacious.) Trousers down I plonked myself on the seat. Cheap plastic one this, not as nice as my old wooden friend but still a thousand times better than that cursed Connington thing.

As I sat I stewed and brooded and worked myself up into a bit of a rage. How dare she? Sounds foolish to you, perhaps;

and it does to me, looking back. But when you're retired it's the little things that get to you. Some end up writing apoplectic letters to the *Daily Mail*. I hadn't got to that stage, yet.

So when Freya came home she was hardly through the door before I set on her. "What in blazes have you done? Where's the old seat?"

She brushed past me and plonked her briefcase on the kitchen table. "I threw it away."

"What?!" I felt my temples throb. "There was nothing wrong with it!"

"It was old and manky and we've got a new one now."

"You know what I think about that!"

She frowned and seemed about to shout at me, but then she laughed. "Brian Logan, you really are a silly man at times! It's only a loo seat!"

"Well I don't like it, and I'm not going to use it."

She put her hands on her hips. "Going to use Trap Two, are we? What, even in the depths of winter?"

"Even in the depths of winter," I rumbled. My guts also rumbled. "What's for tea?"

"Chicken madras."

"Excellent!" I loved a good curry and Freya was a damned good cook.

We enjoyed the curry with a bottle of Rioja and a good DVD and retired to bed early as per. Freya read her Kindle for a bit whilst I dropped off almost right away. Always been a sound sleeper. Only problem is weak bladder. Need to get up and pee a few times a night during the small hours.

And so it was that night.

I woke from a dream to see three o' clock in glowing slightly blurry green digits on the bedside clock. That urgent feeling that cannot be ignored made itself known. Still half asleep I sat up and swung out of bed, sitting on the edge for a sec. Dangerous to leap straight up out of bed, especially at my age. Didn't bother with the light, knew the way, even in pitch darkness. Shuffled out of bedroom across landing into bathroom. Always slept in birthday suit so just lifted lid and plonked myself straight down on seat. Seemed strangely warm.

I started to go at exactly the same moment that I realised. Realised where I was sitting. I jerked upwards in revulsion but then slumped back down as I was still going. I squirmed and grimaced in discomfort and the moment it is was all over I almost leapt off the damned seat. I pulled the light cord and look down. The vile, heathen colours of the inscriptions on the seat almost seemed alive in the sudden luminescence, writhing and cavorting in bacchanalian abandon.

The skin on my buttocks itched and burned. A sharp pain sliced right across my abdomen and I almost cried out, but then it was gone. I stumbled back to bed, grumbling and vowing to get rid of that vile seat first thing in the morning.

I had strange dreams that night, about a tall woman with a pale face and stern green eyes. She was trying to tell me something, but I couldn't hear or understand her.

The morning came, and with it the most awful pains in my guts. Right from my chest down into my bowels, a dreadful throbbing stabbing sensation. I got up and got dressed and took some Collis Browne's, usually did the trick when I had this sort of thing.

But not this time.

Over breakfast, which I didn't feel like eating at all, I suddenly felt the urgent need for a number two. I stood and made for the stairs – then, remembering, I changed direction and went outside to Trap Two, walking very quickly and trying to hold it back. I thrust open the door of Trap Two only to be met with a scene of utter disaster. The floor was awash with water, and the bowl full to the brim! As I watched there was a desolate glugging sound and more water surged over the top and onto the lino.

Things were getting rather desperate down below, and, feeling the hand of fate closing around me, I half-ran, half-walked back into the house, got up the stairs somehow, downed trousers and plonked myself on the damned gyppo seat. The lurid hieroglyphs thereupon seemed to burn into the flesh of my buttocks.

It wasn't a moment too soon. My bowels opened and I passed a great volume of liquid. It came out like a flock of sparrows. The pain in my guts went immediately and I sighed with immense relief.

I cleaned myself up and flushed the mess away, and took a moment to regain my dignity. I was about to go back downstairs when the pain returned. It was like being run through with a rapier. And the need to go came back with an urgency I could scarcely believe possible. Almost tearing my trousers and pants down I sat again--the symbols burning hotter now--and emptied myself once more. I remained sitting after, wary of moving from the seat despite my great distaste for it, and sure enough a few minutes later came the next wave. Afterwards I slumped on the seat, head in my hands, feeling totally drained.

There was a knock on the door. "Are you all right?"

"No!" I exclaimed. "Your dratted curry... it's given me the bloody shits!"

A note of concern entered Freya's voice. "There's blood?!"

"No, no, just... oh God." It came again. I waited a full five minutes before cleaning up and going downstairs. Freya sat at the kitchen table, concern in her hazel eyes.

"I'll be OK," I muttered.

"It can't be my curry," she said. "I'm all right. It's probably your IBS playing up again."

"Probably," I sighed. I suddenly felt very tired, and the pain in my guts started up again, accompanied by a bubbling, churning feeling deep inside. "Oh Jesus Christ," I moaned, and headed upstairs once more as quickly as I could.

This time I didn't quite make it and I am afraid I let myself down.

Freya was sympathetic and took my trousers to the washing machine as I sat there, passing great volumes of watery diarrhoea, feeling the most wretched I have ever felt in my life.

And the skin on my arse was red raw. I had to get off this cursed seat! But I couldn't.

I felt as weak as a kitten and dizzy as a dervish. I leaned my elbows on my legs and realised I was shivering and shaking. The smell was awful. Even after I'd flushed, I could still taste it in my mouth. The horrid thing was that it didn't smell like faeces, not at all – it smelt like something dead, as if my insides were rotting away and I was shitting them out. Oh God! What if this was it? What if I were dying?

I took a deep sobbing breath and inadvertently sucked the foul smell into my lungs. I immediately began to heave. I slid off the toilet and onto my knees and retched heavily into the toilet bowl, my eyes watering like hell and my innards feeling as if they were being squeezed by a giant fist. I truly thought I was doing to die, but the spasms passed, and I just knelt there, elbows on the seat, panting, my face sheened in sweat. And then came another wave. It happened so quick I didn't have time to get up and get back on the toilet, so I am afraid I embarrassed myself quite badly. All over the wicker Ali Baba washing-basket opposite the loo.

And then, for a short period, it was all over. I retired to bed, where I lay shivering and sweating, on the borders of delirium.

Freya took the Ali Baba basket into the garden, clothes and all, and burned it. I tried to shout from the bedroom that she should take the gyppo seat and burn that too, but my voice was just a throaty rasp.

I don't like to remember the rest of that day. The stomach pains would start, build and build until I had to get out of bed and stagger to the loo and sit myself on that accursed seat. Relief would come as scalding fluid jetted down into the bowl, the pain would subside and I would return to bed. Repeat every half an hour for the whole day.

I tried ripping the seat off but the damned thing would not budge, it was as if it had fused into place. That or I was too weak to shift it.

I couldn't keep anything down. Slice of dry toast was all I could manage, and it came out like it went in, almost intact. Freya was a great nurse, taking the day off work to look after me, making sure I drank enough water to replace the fluid I lost. Of course, I exhorted her time and time again to get rid of the confounded Connington but she'd just smile indulgently. I also pleaded with her to swap the seat for the one in Trap Two but she flatly refused.

"That blasted seat is cursed!" I gibbered. "We have to get rid of it!"

"Don't be silly, I've been using it too and I'm perfectly okay."

She did, however, call a plumber to have a look at Trap Two but he wasn't due to arrive until the next day. So on the Connington I was forced to ride.

Night fell and with it some relief from the torment in my bowels.

I was tormented instead by strange dreams.

I see the woman with dark hair and green eyes again, standing smoking a ciggy, leaning against the door of a static caravan. She seems to be deep in thought. Then I'm inside the caravan, watching over her shoulder as she paints symbols onto something with deft, delicate strokes. I try to cry out and she turns and smiles at me, those green eyes flashing. Then I am in a kitchen, large and expensive-looking, as a different woman with long blonde hair and blue eyes, quite a beauty, unwraps a large rectangular parcel. When she sees what's inside she smiles radiantly. Then I am outside, in a cemetery. A funeral is taking place. The blonde-haired woman is amongst the mourners, her beautiful face dimmed by grief. Someone taps me on the shoulder. I turn and it is the green eyed woman again. A voice is whispering in my ear, a voice cold and dry as autumn leaves: Maibh Maginn... Maibh Maginn... She is watching the funeral from a distance under the shade of a yew tree. Then Maibh and I are outside her caravan and she is talking and gesturing with great animation, but I can't catch what she's saying.

Then I woke up with the terrible griping pains again. I get back on the toilet, on the cursed Connington, voiding my bowels and the symbols that Maibh has painted are burning, burning into my flesh and as I shit myself empty I know what has to be done.

***

In the morning, I'm feeling somewhat better. In my mind, Maibh's green eyes seemed to watch over me, and in my guts, the pain had died down into a gentle fluttering. I managed to make it down to breakfast, though I wasn't risking eating anything just yet.

"I don't lay down the law often but were getting rid of that seat."

"Brian, don't be silly. There's nothing wrong with it."

I wasn't about to tell Freya about the dream or Maibh Maginn. "Please, Freya! I'm not asking, I am telling. We are getting rid of it. We can't burn it, it won't burn." (How I knew this I didn't know - was that what Maibh was telling me in the dream?). I licked my lips and leaned across the table towards Freya. "We have to make a gift of it. We can give it to your sister." I immediately realised that even though I disliked Lotte there was no way I would wish my sufferings on her. I held up a hand. "No – we'll just take it to a charity shop."

Freya regarded me as if I'd just sprouted antlers. "This isn't because I got it at a car booty, is it?"

"No."

"Then why? It's only IBS, and you seem better now."

"Freya, please just indulge me. Put it down to the whim of a dotty old man."

Freya began clearing the breakfast things away. Eventually she agreed, but only because I'd been so ill and if getting rid of the toilet seat would make me feel better then so be it.

And that was the end of the cursed Connington. Freya removed it from the upstairs loo (had a hell of a time doing this and had to saw through the bolts), took it to Scope and returned with a plain wooden one from B&Q. Whilst she was out the plumber called and fixed Trap Two. Just in time. I spent the rest of the morning in there, letting the illness take its course, and thinking back over things.

I thought of the dream. I thought of Maibh Maginn. Who was the blonde woman? Who had died, and how? I decided some things were better off not knowing.

I had been sitting for an hour and a half without any pain or attack of the trots, and I realised that I was cured.

And that was the end of it. Or so I thought.

***

A few weeks later, I came down to breakfast to find Freya standing at the kitchen window, staring out at the garden.

"Cup of tea?" I offered.

Freya shook her head.

"Breakfast?"

No response.

"You've not been eating much of late, my dear. And you've lost weight..."

The words died in my mouth as she turned to face me. Her hazel eyes met mine and I knew immediately. I went to her and held her and she sobbed. I tried not to cry myself. Had to be strong for her now.

She died three months later.

So now I live alone, in this big house with all my memories. Thought of selling up and getting a smaller place, but I don't want to leave the place Freya and I shared so many happy years together. I get lots of visitors, and the children visit every week, so I am never really alone.

I tried to find Maibh Maginn, even employed a private investigator, no luck. I went to Scope but the Connington wasn't there.

So if you or someone you know comes across the cursed, vile thing, I advise you to get rid of it ASA bloody P. Make a gift of it. Give it to someone you don't like. Sent it to the tax man. But for God's sake don't sit on the bloody thing. Not even for a minute.

Blood on Santa's Claw
by Richard Freeman

It was early September when Dave Popple, store manager at Smedley & Sons, noticed the wisp of red tinsel on the ceiling of the toy department. The offending item must have been there since last Christmas, hidden away in the corner like a bit of gaudy spider's web. He would normally have told one of the floor staff to remove it but the tinsel insulted his aesthetic tastes so much he climbed up onto a chair and pulled it down himself. He hated the feel of the stuff against his skin and quickly shoved it into his pocket, making a mental note to tell the cleaning staff to be a bit more diligent in future.

Dave hated Christmas. He hated the tacky, down-market decorations the owners insisted on putting up each year. He hated the bunting. He hated the plastic reindeer with their moronic staring eyes. He hated the poorly-made grotto. He hated the fat, half-cut Father Christmas in his cheap fancy dress costume. He hated the stupid looking elves in their tights and pointy ears and most of all he hated the music.

What on earth made Old Mr Smedley think people wanted to hear such dross? It was bad enough for the shoppers but staff had to stomach it for eight-hour shifts. Dave always thought it was a miracle that the music didn't drive him bonkers and turn him into a serial killer. He recalled thinking that last year, if he ever had to listen to Wham's '*Last Christmas*' one more time, he would start killing customers and dressing up in their skins.

It seemed that each year Christmas tat was creeping into the shops earlier and earlier. They had not started putting up the Halloween displays yet, but Dave didn't doubt that the first retarded-looking snowmen would beat any of the ghosts or monsters to the shelves.

By contrast he loved Halloween. It seemed to have none of the crass commercialism or stomach turning saccharin of Christmas. His memories of Halloween were boyhood adventures. Trick-or-treating dressed up as a Cyberman or

Frankenstein's monster. Creeping round 'haunted' houses with friends on ghost hunts - nothing was ever found of course. The houses were just derelict but the thrill was real.

Christmas brought presents but it also brought the cold, annoying carols, rubbish television, visits to his stuffy Great Aunt in Bridlington, badly-knitted sweaters and horrid looking, tacky decorations. Worst of all were the nativity plays at school. Kids dressed as barnyard animals forgetting their lines whilst the popular kids played Joseph and Mary (with a baby doll Jesus), the wise men and the angels. An hour's worth of preachy bollocks, just what every kid wanted to sit through.

Dave pushed the thought of the vile season out of his head and walked back to his office. The incident was forgotten by the time the store closed and Dave drove home. He had been mulling over sales figures, new interns and the 'Back to School' window displays on the journey. He parked the car in the garage and trudged up the path to his front door.

As per his evening ritual he dropped his briefcase on the hall table, made a fuss of Spit, his Scottie dog, shouted a hello to his wife, Sandra, and bent down to slip off his shoes.

There, coiled around his left shoe, like a tiny, glittery feather boa was the tinsel. It must have fallen out of his pocket when he took out his car keys. "Bloody stuff," he snarled under his breath and unwound the tinsel. He took it into the kitchen and threw it into the pedal bin.

"What's that darling?" asked Sandra looking up from the casserole she was making.

"Just a bit of tinsel. Found it at work today. It must have been there since last year."

"What was it doing on your boot?"

"Well I pulled it down and stuffed it in my pocket. I was going to bin it but I forgot. It must have fallen out and got tangled round my shoe."

The evening was pleasant enough. They had a nice dinner, took Spit for a walk through the park and ended up in the Saucy Pig for a few pints. Spit played with the landlord's Jack Russell before they wandered home and Sandra went off to bed. Dave stayed up a while longer watching a documentary about New Wave music on BBC Four.

Something shiny caught Dave's eye in the corner of the room. That bastard tinsel again! Somehow it had gotten out of the pedal bin and into the living room. Spit must have pulled it out of the bin, the little bugger. He hadn't turned out the bin since he was a puppy.

Dave picked up the tinsel. It seemed longer than he remembered. He realised that Spit was curled up on the bed with Sandra. Dave went into the back yard and set fire to the tinsel with his fag lighter. It caught alight and burned easily. He felt a satisfaction looking at the multi-coloured flames that consumed it.

"Must be East European shit, burns like fuck."

A slight breeze blew the ashes into the night and Dave went back indoors and locked the door.

The next day, he was walking through the Food Hall when he stopped dead. There in front of him were a row of Christmas puddings. They were not the standard supermarket type, shaped like flat-topped mountains or tiny volcanoes, but the traditional spherical ones. Each was the size of a football and topped with icing and a sprig of holly. The puddings had not been there the day before and he was unaware of any delivery.

"Oi, Tina," he shouted to one of the staff, "when did these puddings come in?"

Tina walked over the look on her face made it obvious that she was as surprised as he was.

"I've no idea Mr Popple. They weren't here this morning and I can't recall a delivery. It's a bit early for Christmas puds as well don't you think?"

"Way too early Tina. I think there must have been a mix up. I'll ask around."

None of the other staff knew where the puddings had come from. No one had signed for them and everyone swore there had been no deliveries that morning. Dave rang around the various supply companies but none had delivered to

Smedley & Sons that morning. Annoyed, Dave had them taken off the shelves and put in storage.

Driving home that night Dave switched on the car radio and was appalled to hear Wizzard's *'I Wish it Could be Christmas Every Day'*.

"Jesus, summer's only just over and already they're putting this shit on the wireless!"

He fiddled with the knob searching through the static for another station. Slade's *'Merry Xmas Everybody'* blared out of the speaker, causing Dave to swear and wince simultaneously. He desperately turned the dial again and was rewarded with Cliff Richard's vomit-inducing *'Mistletoe and Wine'*. He switched the wireless off in disgust and slipped on a CD of Joy Division. By the time he had reached home he had calmed down.

Back at home he saw there were several letters address to him on the hall table. He opened them. Each and every one was a Christmas card. Tacky grinning Father Xmases leered out at him together with poorly-painted Victorian urchins with oversized heads and doe eyes. None of the senders had put their names inside.

"Sandra, come and look at this." He waved the cards.

"Christmas cards? Who the hell would be sending Christmas cards in September?" she said.

"I think it's someone's idea of a bad joke," he mumbled.

Sandra looked at the envelopes.

"These postmarks are from all over the ockey, Leeds, Edinburgh, Paignton."

"I'm beginning to think that bloody Christmas is haunting me." Dave sloped off to the fridge and got himself a beer.

Back at work the next day all seemed fine until Dave went to the canteen. Turkey and trimmings were on the menu along with mince pies. His stomach turned over. He hated the dry tasteless meat. A great feathered swindle he had always thought.

Later that afternoon in the Sports Department Alan Jarold, the department head, was walking blithely round in a hideous knotted sweater. The chunky, ill-fitting garment featured a number of reindeer trotting through the snow and some poorly-rendered fir trees. He looked like a complete arse and on top of that he was flouting the shop dress code.

He swiftly checked that no customers were about then strode over.

"Alan, what the hell have you got on. Is this a joke?"

"No Dave," he answered, "I just thought it might be nice to wear it for once. My Nan knitted it for me years ago."

"What were you thinking man?" barked Dave. "You know there's a damn dress code and besides its months to Christmas. Now get it off and put your jacket back on."

Alan grudgingly pulled the ugly sweater off, looking like a chagrined schoolboy, then slunk off.

"And don't let me catch you in it again."

Dave looked around the food section. Thankfully there was no more Christmas-related fare on the shelves but the mystery of the plum duffs and their origin remained. For some reason he felt compelled to check on them. He wandered down to storage and unlocked the door.

There they were, all in a row on the shelf, save for one that must have rolled off and fallen to the floor. The pudding had split in half.

On closer inspection there was a trail of crumbs and raisins leading away from it towards a ventilation grille that looked like it had been broken.

"Rats, that's all I need on top of everything else. Now I'll have to call Rentokil in."

That night Dave dreamed that a huge length of red tinsel was winding about him like some constricting snake, choking the life from him in its garish coils. He awoke in a cold sweat with visions of a festive anaconda swallowing him whole.

To his horror the Christmas invasion had grown in strength the following day. Now loops of tinsel hung from the roofs of every floor. *'Last Christmas'* was playing instead of the classical music usually piped into the store. Hillary, the fifty-year-old with the orange tan and skin like old leather from Cosmetics, accosted Dave and held up a sprig of mistletoe. He shoved her away in disgust. He saw more members of staff with red and white Christmas hats on their heads. Were they all in on this? Was it some kind of vast conspiracy against him? He was a good boss, fair, generous with bonuses. He never mentioned the appalling haircut sported by Keith in the Sports Department or the misspelt tattoos adorning the arms of Barry from Hardware. What had he done to deserve this?

Then he saw the abomination in the middle of the store. A twenty-five-foot Christmas tree covered in baubles, tiny regency soldiers, golden angels, stars and crown with a Disneyesque fairy of stomach-turning cuteness.

He should have been bellowing with rage but he felt weak, dizzy. He staggered down to Women's Wear. Angel Blake would help him. She was head of the department, sensible and hot to boot. Dave had always secretly fancied her, she wore open-toed shoes and Dave had a real foot fetish. In summer she was known to go barefoot. Dave shook himself and concentrated on the matter at hand.

There she was at her station; dressed sensibly in the store jacket and dress, long blond hair falling to her shoulders.

"Hi Mr Popple, can I help you?"

"Thank goodness Angel, the whole store seems to have gone mad. Who the hell is behind all this Christmas rubbish?"

As Angel leaned forwards Dave noticed something. Angel was wearing pointed rubber elf ears. She grinned inanely as he backed away. Dave made a run for his office past dopey-looking plastic reindeer, shelves of nativity snow-globes and stacks of empty cardboard boxes wrapped to look like presents. Once inside he locked the door.

With shaking hands he rang head office and blurted out his story. A calm voice answered.

"Not to worry Mr Popple. We will have someone down to sort this out ASAP."

He slumped at his desk and took a slug of whiskey from a little bottle he kept in his desk drawer. Then he remembered its association with Yuletide and tossed it back into the drawer. He stayed in his office for the next half hour. Even from behind the closed door he could hear the ghastly Christmas hits being played around the store. It seemed now that the staff were doing the conga. In his mind's eye he could see them snaking between the displays. Dave was now fearing for his sanity.

Sometime later there was a knock at his office door. Dave opened it an inch and sheepishly peered through. A tall man dressed in black stood at the door. He had black hair, greying at the temples and a black beard. His demeanour was somewhat saturnine and he reminded Dave of Roger Delgado who played *The Master* in the 1970s *Dr Who*. He held a black briefcase.

"Mr Popple?"

Dave nodded.

"My name is Damian Golightly. Head Office sent me. I'm here to help with your problem."

Dave ushered Mr Golightly in to the office and began to explain. The bearded man held up a hand.

"I have been briefed on the details. First things first. I need to see the puddings."

Dave gave him a blank look.

"The Christmas puddings man! I need to see them post-haste."

A confused Dave lead Mr Golightly to the store room where the unaccounted-for puddings had been left. Golightly rushed over and examined them closely.

"Thank god, only one has hatched so far."

"Hatched?"

"These are Santa eggs. A whole batch of them." He swiftly opened his briefcase and took out a hammer. He struck the nearest pudding and it exploded in a shower of sultanas and orange zest. Something was wriggling like an oversized, gaily-coloured maggot in its centre. It looked like a red and green stocking, the old-fashioned kind kids used to hang by the fireside in the days before PlayStations. It seemed animated like a sock puppet and turned to snap at Golightly savagely. He proceeded to bludgeon it with the hammer until it lay still.

"That was the larval form of a Father Christmas. A few days more and it would have hatched. Gorging itself on Christmas kitsch it would have built itself a grotto, in which it would have transformed into a full-grown Santa. Quick we have to destroy the others too."

He handed Dave another hammer and between them they smashed a further thirty Santa eggs and killed the stocking larva within. Dave was horrified at the thought of another thirty of these writhing monsters getting loose in the store and pupating. At least now they were only dealing with one.

Golightly turned to Dave.

"Your atavistic horror of Christmas is well-founded. Christmas is a force, an entity. Our research suggests that it may even predate mankind."

"Your research? Who are you?"

"I'm a Santa Slayer, a Christmas Hunter. We are an elite group who are brought in to tackle the breaches when Christmas breaks through. Christmas is inherently evil and it has the patience of Job. It exists in the black, howling voids between worlds and times but it is ever scratching at the door and seeking an entrance. In recent years it has been growing stronger. When Christmas breaks through it will manifest on the physical plane. At first its influence is low. It appears as tinsel or tacky Christmas decorations but it soon grows in power. A fully-fledged Father Christmas in his grotto is the ultimate manifestation. We have to put an end to this nightmare now."

The thought of such a cavalcade of horror and perversion loose in his store made Dave feel sick. "But how can we fight such a thing?"

"You use water to douse a fire. All things have their opposites and the opposite of Christmas is Halloween."

"We have Halloween decorations in storage. They were due to go up next month."

"I think Mr Popple that Halloween will be coming early to Smedley & Sons."

Sometime later two men in fancy dress crept through the aisles of the store. Dave was dressed as the Wolfman and Golightly as Dracula. Each carried a trick-or-treat bag and a pumpkin-shaped torch. Golightly clutched a witch's broom in his free hand. Despite the absurdness of the situation, Dave was scared. His dislike of Christmas had grown now into a full-blown fear.

Dave had managed to cut the main wire in the speaker control room so that the vile Christmas music had been silenced. But a fresh hell awaited them. There beside the Christmas tree was a grotto decorated with snowmen and winter scenes of children skating and having snowball fights.

"He's grown faster than I could have imagined" hissed Golightly. "An adult Santa will be waiting in there for us."

Suddenly from all sides, members of staff emerged. All dressed as elves with plastic ears, pointy hats with bells, curly shoes and ridiculous green tights.

"Christmas has the power to affect those around it, warping and changing them. They are Santa's slaves now," whispered Golightly.

The crowd drew closer, grinning like imbeciles. Golightly raised his pumpkin torch and switched it on. The Christmas elves drew back hissing. Dave followed suit and tossed some rubber bats at them, causing the elves to scatter and run off down the aisles like rabbits.

"Well done," said Golightly, "but now we must enter the heart of darkness itself."

The bold Santa Slayer kicked open the grotto door. The inside was a lurid red, lit by the glowing electric nose of a plastic Rudolph. Mounds of wrapped gifts lined the sides of the grotto alongside leering animatronic snowmen with icicle fangs, drunkenly lolling polar bears and above it all, a great web of tinsel. At the centre of this Hieronymus Bosch style vision, on a red and gold throne sat the fiend himself, Santa Claus.

A bloated approximation of the human form, its booted, chubby legs seemed too small to support its vast bulk. The thing seemed to be comprised of rolls of fat clad in white-trimmed red velvet with a matching cape. An elongated red hat with a white pompom sat atop the hideous head. Tiny, black, beady eyes that reminded Dave of currants in dough, glittered malevolently above the ruddy nose and cheeks. The mouth was twisted into a sardonic grin that showed row upon row of predatory teeth. Below them trailed a long white beard whose strands seemed to move with an unsettling, ophidian life.

"HO HO HO," it boomed. The sound seemed to penetrate right through Dave, rattling his teeth.

"I am Father Christmas, I am Santa Claus, I am Père Noel, I am Kris Kringle, I am Saint Nicholas. I am all these things and many, many more. I bid you welcome to my grotto."

Both men raised their Halloween torches and shone them at the beast but the orange light was diffused by the red.

"A paltry effort gentlemen," roared the Santa.

The fronds of its trailing beard rose up like cobras and began to grow longer with un-natural speed. Before Golightly or Dave could dodge them they whipped around the men like pallid tentacles. The pair were swept off their feet and dragged along the floor. Hoisted up they dangled upside down before the Santa's face with its Cheshire cat grin.

"I've checked my list, twice mind, twice, and you have been NAUGHTY!"

Father Christmas opened its maw impossibly wide showing the legion of fangs that sprouted therein. Dave wriggled one hand free and tossed a fistful of white chocolate skulls into the Santa's mouth. The brute gagged and foamed and the tenticular beard loosened its grip slightly. Golightly shone his torch directly into the evil little eyes that glittered like pips of jet.

"Girls and boys won't get any toys," it howled. The beard flung Golightly aside and he crashed into a mountain of cheap gifts. The deadly white locks focused on Dave now, winding tighter and tighter.

Dave fought desperately and with his waning breath shouted, directly into the monster's face, "Trick or Treat!"

Father Christmas drew back hissing. Golightly had emerged from the present pile and was marching forward with a determined look on his face.

"In the name of Godzilla, The Beast from 20,000 Fathoms, the Daleks and The Creature from the Black Lagoon, I cast thee out."

He sprayed silly string spider webs into Santa's face temporarily blinding him.

"By Cushing, Lee and Price, I bind thee."

The obese horror squirmed at the words but seemed unable to move. Golightly continued his incantation.

"Kolchak, Pertwee, Quatermass, Baker, Harryhausen."

Santa foamed like a rabid dog. Golightly picked up the witch's broom. Dave saw he had sharpened the handle. The Santa Slayer raised the broom on high and brought it down with all the force he could muster into the abomination's chest.

The great sack that was Santa's bloated body seemed to deflate, falling in on itself as he screamed and howled. The collapsing maw vomited forth polystyrene snowflakes as it began to lose its shape.

"Ho-Ho-ho-ho-h....."

Saint Nick was dissolving like ice under sunlight as they looked. The very fabric of the grotto seemed to be coming apart as the walls and roof sagged. Both men ran from the lair and as they looked back they saw it fall like a pack of soggy cards and vanish.

Likewise the tree and the other decorations melted away like a bad dream; the staff, sans elf costumes, were looking around in a confused manner.

Back in the office both men had a stiff drink, gin this time not whiskey. Dave's legs felt like jelly but Golightly didn't seem fazed.

"How can I thank you Mr Golightly?"

The tall man smiled. "No need my friend. Being a Santa Slayer is a vocation, a calling if you will. To have destroyed evil is enough. Besides the company are paying me through the nose."

Golightly shook Dave firmly by the hand. "I must be moving on now. Christmas never rests. It will try again elsewhere." With that he turned and left the office.

Later that day, Dave Popple went to a travel agents and bought a three-week holiday in Sri Lanka to run right over the Christmas period.

Road Rage
by David Croser

"Thank God for that."

Keshia eased the car past the artic and slipped back into the left-hand lane.

Behind her she could hear Volney mumbling and whining, a sure sign he was waking up. The twins didn't help, arguing over their Gameboys – plural – what one wanted the other had to have.

"Mum. Are we there yet?"

"No."

"Well how much longer?"

"Soon. We'll get there soon."

Keshia glanced at Ryan, dozing despite the noise from the back.

His idea, this weekend to Brighton.

"It'll bring us together, babe. Make us see what we'd be losing."

How much love could you have, could you give, before it ran thin, colourless?

What would I be losing if I took me and the kids back to Tulse Hill instead of your crummy council flat in Edmonton?

Keshia missed South London, taking the kids down Brockwell Park of a Sunday afternoon, mum and family on the doorstep. North of the river, everything seemed greyer, grimier and nastier. Ryan's place overlooked the North Circular with its abiding theme of sirens and horns, the air like iron filings in the throat. She was scared for the kids, for their future.

What would I be losing?

The only man who's ever loved me, treated me right, respected me, taken on another man's kids and treated them as his own. But a bone-idle sod, workshy, getting a pittance from the Social while I'm sitting weekends and nights in a sweaty box of a minicab office for cash in hand. Sure he cooked, cleaned (after a fashion), watched the kids. But he drinks, and when he drinks he vanishes for hours, days sometimes, leaving me with everything. Then he comes back, always with flowers, sweets for the kids, more promises it won't happen again.

"Never, babe."

Like a stuck record, like a loop of time going back on itself, devouring itself, devouring him.

What would I lose?

So I go home to Tulse Hill, could I put up with my mother's face?

That injured martyr's expression, knowing, I told you so. She's never liked Ryan, never seen why her daughter could take up with a white man, and such a bum too.

What would I lose?

Ryan stirred, squinting out at the traffic.

"Where are we, babe?"

"Junction 21. Just past the turn-off for the M1."

"Christ, that all? We got on at Junction 25. We've been on the road for – what – two hours?"

"Your idea, going M25."

"It's a Friday. You know what cross-town traffic's like."

"Mum."

"If we'd left earlier."

"How could we? I couldn't get me giro till ten."

"Mum."

"If you got out of that pit before nine for one you could've queued up like the rest."

"Mum!"

"You know what time we got to bed last night."

"We know why that was – what?!"

"A crash, Mum! Over there!"

Keshia looked. On the hard shoulder just ahead. Traffic in front was slowing already. She could see two vehicles: one red, the other green.

Red was a BMW. Was. A tangle of twisted, steaming metal, screened by flashing lights and uniforms. Even at forty, the instant congealed, thickened into a scene almost frozen, squashed insects trapped in filthy amber. Keshia shuddered, then the moment was gone and the overhead signals warned that the speed limit was down to fifty.

Volney was crying now and the twins had resolved their argument, getting down to some serious fighting, Gameboys twittering and squawking.

And Ryan was dozing off again.

Great.

Junction 13: Staines A30.

Two hours later. Around three in the afternoon, but the battery in her watch was dead and the car clock was missing its minute hand.

Capital Radio burbled on and on about it being a lovely day. She was sure they'd played the same pissing record three times now, but it was hard to tell as the signal seemed to be breaking up.

What did they call this road? Europe's biggest car park. Since passing the accident they had gone from fifty to forty, forty to thirty, thirty to a dead stop.

Keshia thought of *One Foot in the Grave*, the episode where Victor Meldrew and his missus are stuck in a jam like this. What had been hilarious at the time seemed sour now. Sat here, the kids giving it hell, not a breath of wind on a hot day, Keshia could cheerfully have grabbed the car jack from the boot and battered them all to death. And that idle sod still dozing, head lolling to one side, snoring. She had had to open the window if only to let out her own anger, her own frustration.

It hung like a cloud over the road. It hung like a cloud over the road; an old bruise, swollen with the frustration of thousands. It churned, curdled and thickened as they went round and round and round and …

A car horn jerked her awake.

It woke Volney. Ryan too.

"Christ, babe. What's happening?"

Keshia flicked a glance. "Nothing. Go back to sleep."

Nearly fell asleep at the wheel. God. Dear sweet Jesus.

"You needn't say it like that, babe."

Keshia glared at him.

"Like what?"

Ryan looked away. He peered out the windscreen.

"There's services coming up. Why don't we stop for a rest?"

Keshia sipped at a hot black coffee. The twins were off playing on the game machines. Volney was dozing in Ryan's arms. They were sat at a table overlooking the motorway, at a steady sludge of traffic snaking away in both directions. The mid-afternoon heat haze seemed to merge the traffic into one long serpent, each car a scale on its immense body. Keshia turned away and looked at Ryan, hugging her boy, rocking him gently and whispering a lullaby to him. One or two people at adjoining tables glanced across, smiling.

He had that effect on people. For all his faults, people warmed to Ryan. As soon as they walked out of the flat people were stopping, nodding, calling, saying hi as he passed. Everyone knew Ryan. Everyone liked him. Good old Ryan. For all her earlier anger, Keshia felt herself warm towards him.

And love? Oh yes, that too.

It still returned to that, her cycle of rage, anger and frustration with him.

"How long d'you reckon we've got left to go, babe?" Ryan asked, settling Volney in his lap and sipping at his tea.

Keshia shook her head, glancing across the café for a clock. There, above the cashier. According to it the time was half-past ten. The second hand was stuck. You'd think they'd fix it.

"Feels about four. What time you say Jody's expecting us?"

Ryan grinned lopsidedly. "Time's not an issue."

Keshia finished her tea. "Or cleanliness, or having a lock on the front door, or keeping track of who's staying at that bloody commune of his."

Ryan shrugged. "He's an old mate. It's not costing us nothing. It'll be cool, you'll see."

Keshia stood up. "If we ever get there. Go and grab the twins."

Junction 10: London (SW) Guilford A3.

Keshia could see the man in front of her industriously picking his nose.

He was having a real good go at it, index finger up to the first knuckle, staring obliviously out at the rest of the jammed-up traffic around them. The late afternoon (she supposed) sun glared in at them. On the dashboard by her left hand a little fan swung back and forth, not so much cooling them as pushing the slow, heavy heat around. It was plugged into the lighter socket and at least it kept Ryan from lighting up. Not that it would be a cigarette, either.

"Why the hassle, babe? It's part of your culture." At least the fan worked. The radio, as well as the clock, had given up.

So had she. The next junction was with the A24. If they came off there they could follow it up through Epsom and back through the city to Edmonton. This time of day they'd be going against the traffic and …

"Mum. We're moving again."

Keshia pulled herself up smartly, easing off the clutch and moving forward.

She glanced in the mirror at the twins. They were looking bright and cheerful; a lot better than they had been when Ryan dragged them away from the games machines at the service station.

"It was dead cool, Ryan. They had old stuff like Pacman and Space Invaders and this dead-old tennis game."

She couldn't give up. The Brighton turn-off was only two junctions away now.

Junction 4: Bromley A21 Orpington A224.

Keshia shook Ryan awake with her spare hand.

"Look."

"Look? At what, babe?"

"At the sign coming up."

Ryan squinted out, shielding his eyes against the afternoon sun.

"Shit."

He looked at her. "How did we …?"

"We didn't."

"Brighton's off junction seven, babe."

Keshia shot an angry glance at him. "The last junction we passed was nine."

"It can't have been, babe."

"I've just seen it, Ryan. Ten minutes ago: Leatherhead and Dorking on the fucking A24."

Keshia sighed, and glanced back at the kids. "Sorry. But I know what I saw."

Ryan looked at his hands, and put one on Keshia's thigh.

"It's this road, babe. Does it to you sometimes. One big confusing merry-go-round, yeah? We been going for hours. You been driving for hours. One junction seems like another and …"

The car was slowing and Ryan could see flashing lights ahead. Traffic cops waving cars past an accident, making sure people didn't stop and gawp.

Sure enough, the traffic was stopping and gawping. Keshia cursed and swerved out into the middle and then the outer lane, putting her foot down.

"A green car," said one of the twins.

"Red one too," said the other.

Junction 28: Chelmsford A12 Brentwood A1023.

"This is weird," Ryan murmured.

Keshia flicked on the indicator. "It's not me falling asleep then."

Ryan bit his lip. "To get to here we should've gone over the Dartford Bridge. We've only just passed the A2. Sorry, babe."

They pulled into the exit lane.

"We get on the A12 and head back home, yeah?"

"Ryan, look."

Ryan looked, and saw that they were still on the motorway.

"You missed it."

"It wasn't there, Ryan."

Ryan stared at her, looked behind them.

"I saw the countdown signs for the exit. We passed them, but there was no exit."

Ryan looked at light blinking on the dashboard. "We're gonna need to stop soon, babe."

Keshia looked at the low-fuel warning.

"Mum. Where are we?"

Services.

Keshia and Ryan sat in the service station café nursing coffees between them.

They'd found a high chair for Volney, and the twins were finishing off fish fingers and chips. Around them was the noise and bustle of other people doing the same.

"Ryan, I'm scared."

Ryan squeezed her hand. "There's got to be some reason for all this, babe. Mebbe we're all tripping."

"Tripping?" She glared at him.

Ryan shrugged. "Well ... confused, disorientated. We've been on the road for a long time and ..."

"How long have we been driving for Ryan, eh? Come on – tell me."

Ryan looked around; saw a clock over the cashier's desk.

"It's broken," said Keshia. "Just like the one at the last services we stopped at."

Ryan patted her hand. "Ok, babe. Cool. I'll just ask someone."

She gripped his hand fiercely. *"Don't you dare leave us."*

Ryan pulled his hand away and leaned across to the opposite table.

"The time?" asked the man sitting there.

He glanced as his wrist, then tapped his watch. "Sorry, mate. Must have forgot to wind it."

His wife shook her head. "He's so absentminded like this," she said, and looked at hers. She looked up sheepishly. "I've only gone and done the same. Sorry."

Keshia stood up and reached for Volney.

"Come on you two," she said.

"Babe, what're you ...?"

"Getting out of here."

"Why? The kids haven't even finished..."

Keshia leaned towards him, her eyes wide.

"Did you take a look at those two you just spoke to?"

Ryan glanced, embarrassed, at them. Frowned.

"How many people d'you see dressed like that nowadays? How many people still use wind-up watches?"

Grabbing the protesting twins she left the table.

"Look around you, Ryan. Why does this place look exactly the same as the services we stopped at earlier? Do you remember an 'Ouroborous Services' on the M25?" she called back to him.

One or two people glanced up as she stormed out of the café, but most got on with their meals and drinks.

Sure, he thought, there were quite a lot of people dressed funny, in the kinds of clothes his folks - or grandfolks – used to wear, but nobody was acting weird. Except the old dear on the till, who'd tried to charge him eighty-four-and-a-halfpence for their meals and drinks. She'd charged him eighty-five as she said she'd run out of ha'pennies. Apologised for it, too.

Ryan felt suddenly afraid, and hurried out to find his family.

At the garage end of the service station, Ryan made the kids stay in the car when Keshia cried out to him. She was standing by the petrol pumps.

"Well?" she asked, her voice tight. "What do I put in? Four Star's twenty-eight pence a gallon, Two Star's twenty-six pee a gallon."

Ryan stared at the pumps.

"Well, Ryan?" she screamed.

Ryan had taken over the driving. The car was idling by the services exit. Below them traffic snaked away into the twilight.

"So what do we do?" he asked quietly.

"Drive. Get us out of here."

Ryan put the car into gear and was about to pull off when he felt a hand on his shoulder. One of the twins was pointing out the windscreen.

"Ryan, look. Look at the snake."

"What d'you mean, the ..." he said, and followed the boy's arm.

Ryan knew what he was looking at. Despite the failing light he could see the entire six-lane width of the motorway seem to rise up below them.

Some quarter-of-a-mile away it was. The cars, artics, caravans, transits, packed so close together, kept moving, despite the road itself bulging, twisting.

The part of the motorway nearest to them seemed to the motorway nearest to them seemed to have changed, broadened and thickened, and Ryan realised that it resembled the bulge of an immense serpentine head. From either side of its skull, where the hard shoulders should be, two ancient reptilian eyes the size of houses stared at them, glared at them with rage and triumph.

Keshia saw it too, and realised that the traffic on its surface did indeed look like scales on an immense snake.

Faintly, Keshia wondered why the traffic didn't drive off the end of its head, and then she saw it had in its huge mouth the other end of the road, which must be its tail.

Only then did she see how trapped they were, and with that realisation came calmness.

"Let's move. We've got a long way to go."

Keshia eased the car past the artic and slipped back into the left-hand lane.

"Mum. Are we there yet?"

"No."

"Well how much longer?"

"Soon. We'll get there soon."

edited by Stephanie Ellis & S.G. Mulholland

The Thin Dead Line
by O.L. Humphreys

Brown. Mud everywhere. Everything's brown. Not half as chocolaty tasting as it looks.

This was the somewhat un-profound discovery Private Barry Williams had made during his first experience of shelling, and had revisited every one of the countless shellings since. Spitting out mud was a skill every Tommy developed rapidly. To be fair it wasn't just down to the shellings; Williams felt like he hadn't seen any colour other than the brown of soil and the drab green of British fatigues since he'd arrived in this godforsaken corner of Germany. And grey. Plenty of grey. The sky was a constant grey. Either the grey of rain, or the grey of impending rain. The other guys were grey too. Nazi grey.

Cursing, he attempted to wipe grime from the lens of his binoculars with an equally filthy sleeve. Having been tasked with checking up on the Germans manning the Monschau bunkers, Williams was halfway out of the dugout, which was as far as he dared crawl.

"Use your underpants, mate." Lieutenant Norris suggested from within the relative safety of the foxhole. "It's probably the cleanest cloth round here."

"Yeah, but the mud on my pants isn't the type of mud I want getting near my eyes."

Resting on his elbows he raised the binoculars, peered towards the German lines, lowered them, squinted, and then put them back to his eyes. "It looks like they've brought in tankers."

"More tanks?"

"No, it looks like petrol tankers, but with bloody great hoses."

***

It was January 1944. 8th Company had been slowly working its way east through southern Belgium, just north of the border with Luxembourg, moving forward at the snail's pace dictated by the allied line. Most of the action was to the north or south of this particular region, and resources had been moved to where it was needed most. The company was spread thinly.

Then came the reports that the Nazis had initiated what became known as the Ardennes Counteroffensive, taking the Allies by surprise. A covertly-massed German army surged forward into Belgium hoping to obliterate the weakly-defended section of the line of which 8th company formed a small part. Orders from Command HQ were for the horrendously underprepared company to dig in and wait for the wave to hit.

Captain Harrison, exchanged a few awkward words with the men, mainly along the lines of "Give Jerry a bloody good kicking", then retreated to his command tent, where he immediately entered a gin-induced stupor; leaving his lieutenants to organise defence against insurmountable odds.

Two days later Harrison emerged, eyes bloodshot, hands half-raised in surrender, to find the company in much the same state as he had left it. Not a Nazi in sight. The wave of German forces, rather than washing over had washed round them.

A call to Command HQ confirmed that 8th Company was now behind enemy lines. And the line was moving further away by the minute. HQ, realising that the poorly equipped 8th would be better used in disrupting German support than in an all-out rear attack, urged Harrison to continue towards the border and into Germany. There to capture and hold an armoury facility located in the Monschau Forest on the foothills of the Eifel. The Company could take and hold the facility, cutting supplies and hopefully forcing part of the Nazi counteroffensive force to split-off and return back the way they came.

At first there had been excitement as the troops realised that they were finally entering Germany after months of battling through Belgium. When the target was finally sighted through the dense Monschau forest a grim determination gripped the men. The armoury consisted of a complex of concrete bunkers forming part of Hitler's defensive Siegfried Line; however, after a number of disastrous skirmishes the complex proved unyielding. Harrison concluded that actually taking it would be unfeasible for the now heavily depleted 8th company, and they found themselves digging a set of trenches just out of range with the intention of preventing any supplies leaving in the direction of the forces embroiled in the counteroffensive.

The company had been in this unenviable position for over three months. The disruption to the German supplies was a success, not a single truck entered or left the facility. The 8th itself was not forgotten by the main allied army and received its own supplies by airdrop. The standoff lasted until the Allies had finally quashed the Nazi forces in the Ardennes with the unfortunate side effect of forcing the remains of the German army to fall back to the Siegfried Line, encircling the 8th outside the very fortress they were supposed to be laying siege to.

***

Phase One and Two

"Captain?" Norris peered into the Captain's quarters. Captain Harrison had made the cramped shack, which had been hastily built into the wall of the trench, his office and sleeping quarters. It was a dark, cramped space of only about 8 by four feet but the Captain was rarely seen outside of it.

Norris found him lying prone on the floor, one ear to the ground. "Shhhhh ... can you hear that?"

Norris exchanged a knowing glance with Private Jack Powell, who was assigned as assistant to Harrison and now stood on duty outside the bunker. War often affected the minds of the troops in strange ways, but the Captain had been a peculiar one from the outset.

"The blighters are undermining us! I can hear them through the ground!" Harrison frantically looked up at Norris, his moustache quivering with rage. "Get down here, Lieutenant and listen ..."

Norris was unconvinced. "Sir, they have us surrounded. Why would they bother digging under us?"

"That's an order."

"Yes, Captain."

Harrison's large frame already took up most of the filthy floor so with a sigh, Norris got down on all fours under a makeshift writing desk. With a second sigh, he planted his ear in the dirt. And listened ... to the dirt. The dirt was quiet. "Captain, a dozen Nazi tankers have arrived."

"More tanks?"

"No. Petrol tankers, with turrets."

"Shhhh ... I hear something."

This time Norris heard something too; a strange rhythmic droning, more musical than mechanical.

Outside the bunker it had started to rain; however the sound was now audible over the patter of droplets, quickly swelling to a cacophony. Both men lifted their heads from the ground. The sound was coming from outside.

Private Powell burst in. "Captain! It's raining red!"

***

Sergeant Barnbeck waited a respectful distance behind Professor Fahrenkrog as he surveyed the Mercedes tankers firing their toxic, scarlet contents into the air. The musty grey room of the concrete Monschau facility bunker was filled with the sound of classical music, squawking from the overstretched internal-address system, somewhat helping to drown out the din being blasted towards the British. It was Wagner. Naturally.

"We've finally begun, Barnbeck." The Professor didn't move his gaze from the horizontal machinegun slot through which he was observing. "In just a few weeks the cowardly men hiding in the mud out there will form the first battalion of the Glorichen-Verstorbenen."

Sergeant Barnbeck didn't like the sound of it.

"Phase One!" Fahrenkrog held a single finger in the air, eyes still fixed on the scene outside. "Administer a toxin to the subjects to prepare them physically for conscription. This is the necronic which is currently spilling down on them. It will slowly extinguish their lives in the manner required for conscription." A second finger shot up. "Phase Two. While the necronic takes effect, administer visual and aural stimuli to prepare the mind. The rhythms being played all day every day on a three-minute loop will break their spirits, whilst simultaneously disabling all but the most base elements of thought. The red dye in the necronic will compound the effect."

"Just by being red, Professor?"

Professor Fahrenkrog finally turned to face Barnbeck.

The greying professor wore a tweed jacket with a white cotton shirt, his plain green twill trousers were tucked into beige socks pulled up above brown boots. Barnbeck had often mused that the Professor looked very much like he was dressed for a cycling holiday. He did not look impressed.

Picture an unimpressed, tweed-clad cyclist, in a Nazi bunker.

That's how he looked.

"I'll have you know, red is, psychologically, an extremely powerful colour. Blood is red, and the sight of blood is naturally associated with danger. So, on a subconscious level red triggers the emotions associated with danger, including fear, uncertainty and anger. Also, as we are meat eaters and meat is bloody, it also triggers a tendency towards hunger and over consuming. Restaurants, for instance, could sell food quicker if there was a strong red element in their signage and decor. The same applies to over-purchasing of goods too."

"If I owned a shop, placing red labels on my goods would make people buy more?"

Fahrenkrog, tilting his head to one side, gave the concept some thought. "Yes. It would work especially well if combined with wording implying that the product is cheap. Even if it isn't."

"A red discount label would subconsciously affect customers, giving them a hunger to buy things they don't really need, and aren't even reduced in price?" Barnbeck was aghast at the concept.

"Yes, but that would be immoral." Both men nodded sagely in agreement. "Phase Three: we blow the explosives we've planted underneath the British causing them to fall into the cursed catacombs they've unwittingly been camped above. We imprison them there and let whatever godforsaken forces reside in the caverns undo the work of the necronic, resurrecting the British corpses. Remember, it's no good to simply throw in bodies from our own morgues, they need to be fresh: The fire most recently extinguished is more easily rekindled. When they are resurrected the psychological re-profiling we've administered will still be with them ...

"Phase Four. Train them into the Glorichen-Verstorbenen: A brigade of undead fighters to unleash on our enemies."

"It sounds really quite unpleasant."

"For the subjects it will be, as the British say: a bugger."

***

Phase Two

Red, everything's red. The mud is red, the trees are red, even the British uniforms are now red. Norris' skin itched under the gloves he'd not taken off for almost a fortnight and the shirt wrapped round his face made it hard to breath. Plus there was no respite from the droning noise blaring night and day.

The whole company had been heavily exposed to 'The Red' except Lieutenant Norris and Captain Harrison.

When the scarlet rain had started Harrison had ordered Norris to stay in his office area as *Jerry was obviously up to something foul.* They'd relied on the increasingly disgruntled and scarlet-faced Private Powell for information about the state of the troops and supplies, always being careful not to let any of 'The Red' or Powell into the shelter.

At first everyone had assumed they would just keel over, dead from whatever poison the Nazis had sprayed them with. When that didn't happen the troops tried to carry on as normal, but with 'The Red' and 'The Noise' it was impossible. Regular fights started breaking out amongst the company. Everyone felt frustrated, angry and hungry. The term *seeing red* could never be more aptly applied.

Despite Harrison's blustering threats through the barricaded door of the shelter to have everyone involved court marshalled, one attempt was made to concede to the Germans. However that was soon foiled by the ping of a sniper's bullet off the helmet of the Lieutenant carrying the pinkish flag of surrender. The news of this sent the Captain into a second rage on the subject of *Jerry flaunting the rules of engagement*.

Later Powell informed them that one of the company's field chefs had tried serving tomato soup and had been shot.

All red food was now off the menu, having been loaded into mortars by a furious artillery sergeant and volleyed in the direction of 'The Noise'. No Man's Land was peppered with cans of bolognaise and bottled ketchup.

Supplies were almost exhausted as 8th Company had gorged themselves on the remaining food.

Powell eventually stopped visiting the Captain's shelter altogether.

After two weeks of being cooped up in the tiny space, with no intelligent contact from outside, Norris was ordered to cover up in spare clothes so as not to get Red on himself and check what was going on.

By now everyone was too sick to do much at all. Those members of 8th Company that hadn't already expired simply lay comatose on their backs next to those who had, like scarlet corpses waiting for the grave, staring up at the grey sky only the occasional groan or murmur indicating that they were still alive. The Red had drained them of life. Norris felt tempted to join them. Looking at the sky offered some respite from The Red if not The Noise.

At first he'd attempted moving survivors away from their dead comrades, but there were simply too many for him to manhandle on his own and the Captain remained barricaded in his quarters.

So he spent much of his time checking up on the state of the men who were still alive, trying to get them to at least drink a little of what clean water he could find. Before The Red and The Noise the Company had numbered ninety-nine men. Now, including himself, and the Captain there were only twenty three. At every count there were fewer.

This morning he'd witnessed Private Williams rasping his last breath. Now he crouched over Powell desperately listening for a heartbeat.

With a rumble, the ground along the entire British entrenchment collapsed.

***

Phase Three

Coughing and spluttering, Lieutenant Howard Norris ripped the protective gloves from his hands and the shirt from around his face. After some time spent alternately gulping down air and spitting out mud, he decided to seek out Captain Harrison. Finding the Captain, using only the light seeping through the gash in the ceiling of the cavern through which they had fallen, was hard going. He was finally located, mainly by following the sound of cursing about *Jerry*.

At first Norris thought it was a lost cause. The substantial frame of Captain Harrison was firmly wedged under the remains of his own shelter plus no small amount of soil. The sound of his swearing issued from a gap between planks just a finger's breadth wide.

Norris was struggling to lift the Captain's writing desk when Private Powell appeared and wordlessly started tugging at the table. Ribs were clearly protruding from rips in his tunic; Powell did not look well. With much grunting from Norris, moaning from Powell and backed with a plethora of profanities from Harrison the pair of them managed to shift the desk. Norris moved onto the next piece of debris and this time was joined by two more members of 8th Company. By the time Harrison was freed there were twelve groaning men shifting planks and dirt away from the Captain. Many of them had horrific injuries caused by the plummet into the earth, but carried on, seemingly oblivious. Norris was proud that the 8th displayed such pluck in the face of adversity, despite their injuries everyone pulled together to save the Captain. A glowing example of British determination!

Harrison was in a bad way. One knee was a mess of bone and flesh, Norris quickly cleaned and bound it as best he could, tightly tying a strip of cloth above the bloody wound as a makeshift tourniquet, but the Captain was not going anywhere. It was a job for a saw doctor.

The injured man had very little to say except, "I told you so! Bloody Jerry was mining under us all the time!"

Norris turned to survey the scene. More members of 8th Company had joined the group. They milled around aimlessly, not a single word said between them. A new member shuffled his way through the small crowd.

It was Barry Williams.

But Norris had seen Private Williams die.

Something was seriously wrong.

***

Phase Four

Barnbeck peered through the portal-like observation window into the initial cavern of the Monschau catacombs. The window was set in a huge vault-style door, which provided the only entry to the cave system.

He could just make out the indistinct outline of something limping along in the thick ethereal mist which obscured most of the cavern.

Sergeant Barnbeck hoped that this time nothing horrible would suddenly lurch up in front of the portal as it always seemed to.

Suddenly something lurched up in front of the portal.

Barnbeck leapt backwards in fear, almost tripping over Professor Fahrenkrog, who himself was making a rapid retreat. The grotesque scarlet face of a British soldier leered at them from the opposite side, saliva dripping from its slack lips. It made a swift licking motion on the glass with a bloated rotting green-grey tongue, leaving a mess of flesh and spittle, then disappeared as rapidly as it had appeared.

"Why!" Screeched Barnbeck at the window. "Why, always me? You bloody British undead buggers!"

"Ohhh! We're going to have to send someone in to clean that up!" Fahrenkrog exclaimed, clapping his hands excitedly. "I think it's time for Phase Four." Fahrenkrog pressed a button on the internal-address system. "Send down the snatch squad."

"I'm very happy with the numbers, you know. We estimate ninety-nine potential members of the Glorichen-Verstorbenen in there. Ninety-nine is a good number." Fahrenkrog confided as they waited.

"Really?" Barnbeck was unconvinced.

"Yes, ninety-nine as a number creates frustration. It's not quite one hundred, you see? It's not quite there, it's not quite right, it does not sit well with people. Ninety-nine pfennigs is not a mark. If I ask you for ninety-nine pfennigs I've not asked for a mark, but I may as well have done. You see? It causes fear, such an unfriendly number."

Barnbeck was beginning to think everything caused fear.

"It makes people more malleable, they want to get past the ninety-nine. They think they've not paid a mark because they've just paid ninety-nine pfennigs. But the logical part of their brain tells them the ninety-nine may as well be one hundred! It's a truly unsettling number. In our theoretical store I'd price everything with ninety-nine pfennigs at the end. Everyone would think the prices one mark less than they actually were! When combined with the other psychological tools: the effect of scarlet and repetitive rhythms the number ninety-nine can be used to devastating effect ..."

The snatch squad arrived, mercifully cutting Fahrenkrog's musings short. Barnbeck worried that after the war he'd be forced to open a store with the Professor, or worse, a restaurant. A restaurant with a ninety-nine pfennig menu using red signage selling food so fast they'd be unable to maintain any level of quality. All their customers would be angry because of the droning music being played in it and all the red. It would be awful.

"You, private!" Barnbeck halted one of the squad. "Explain this." He indicated to a bandage round the man's head.

"Hit by a can of chopped tomatoes, Sergeant," the private answered with shame in his eyes. "Bloody Tommies."

Sergeant Barnbeck and Professor Fahrenkrog stood back as the huge door swung open and the snatch squad bundled through. "They should be pretty hungry by now," Barnbeck mused.

**

The men's physical state was deteriorating rapidly; they were beginning to rot in the damp environment. In order to keep morale up Norris was trying not to use the 'Z' word around them.

Norris was weak with hunger; the last of the food he had salvaged was gone. He just sat staring at the fire he'd managed to coax to life using the wood which had fallen into the catacombs with them. Waiting for something to happen.

When he'd still had the strength he'd explored part of the cave system and found the massive doorway into the Nazi facility. Creeping up to it he'd popped his head up briefly to glimpse through the window, giving the German officer on the other side, quite a shock.

He'd not had the energy to investigate in the other direction; however a number of the 8th Company seemed to be spending a lot of their time back there.

The Captain had died a few days earlier. Eyes fixed on his ruined leg his last words had been, "When Jerry finally charges, at least I can kick him in the bonce with the other one." Now he was doing surprisingly well, hopping around on his good leg, the other dragging along after him hanging by a strip of flesh and cartilage.

Williams and Powell had had a fight. Williams had attempted to gnaw the rib bones protruding from Powell's uniform. Powell had retaliated by grabbing and pulling the centre of Williams' top lip completely off. Now Williams looked like Adolf Hitler. In reverse. Norris had berated both privates and they wandered off in opposite directions. He hadn't seen either of them since.

***

Sergeant Barnbeck stared through the window in the door to the caves.

There was movement out in the mist. Suddenly something lurched up in front of the portal.

Barnbeck fell back with a curse. "Bloody Hell!"

This time the haggard face at the window had a large section of lip missing, front teeth clearly visible when they should have been covered.

"It's the Inverse Fuhrer!" One of the snatch squad behind him exclaimed. They'd taken to giving the more active undead whimsical nicknames.

The Inverse Fuhrer capered off, back into the fog.

"Throw these ones back in, then prepare for another snatch," Barnbeck ordered.

"I hope we actually get a pop at Inverse Fuhrer or Old Hopper this time," one of the privates whispered as they manhandled each of the crates containing the previously captured British undead back towards the cave entrance.

Sergeant Barnbeck watched with interest as each of the newly-indoctrinated undead angrily thrashed itself free from its respective crate and hobbled off into the catacombs.

***

Norris was slumped close to the fire when he spotted the Nazis looming out of the darkness. With a great effort he managed to pull himself to his feet and tried his best to look dangerous, whilst supported by an outcropping of rock. One of the soldiers was slowly coming straight for him. Norris did a double-take. It was Powell, dressed in a grey German uniform. For a walking corpse he looked quite upset, even a little ashamed. He held his wrists out in front of himself. The bastards had gaffer-taped the Nazi jacket onto him!

The Lieutenant began pulling at the thick black tape, it was impossible to get off without pulling away a fair portion of greyish flesh with it, so he rummaged in his kit for a knife.

Suddenly, with the yell of "Yerrrry!", and at speed which belied the fact he was an overweight corpse with only one working leg, Captain Harrison bowled Private Powell over and the pair started scrapping on the floor. Powell soon got the better of Harrison, straddling the Captain and pounding him with both fists. However a second, then a third deceased soldier ploughed into the fray in aid of the Captain. It seemed the men still had a sense of loyalty as well as hatred for the Nazi uniform.

A similar scene was evolving all round him, with those in Nazi uniform being heavily outnumbered and surrounded by rapidly appearing British-clad undead. Skirmishes were breaking out all around. Norris had to put an end to it before one of them had something serious pulled off. Like a head.

"Everyone disengage! That's an order!" He screamed at the top of his voice, with a few final thumps from the more slowly reacting soldiers, the skirmish was halted.

Using his knife, he cut the Nazi jacket from Powell and made a show of throwing it onto the fire. There was a grunt of approval from Harrison. His leg had finally ripped off and lay discarded on the floor. Norris was surprised to see that it was still twitching.

The other Nazi-clad men similarly had their jackets pulled from them. Untold damage was caused to them in the process. A hand or two was lost to the tape. But at least now they were back to being regular members of the 8th.

It seemed that the sound of the melee had actually bought all of 8th Company back to one spot from wherever they'd been roaming in the further reaches of the caves. Norris figured that as the only surviving member of the company he was now in charge and it was probably best to keep them together in one place. "Fall in men!"

The soldiers formed into rough lines and stood swaying and moaning. The Captain, having some sense that he was above joining in, hopped about before the Company. In what was left of his mind he was taking the Company through their paces on the parade ground, making the occasional *About turn* type noises. Some of the men turned, most didn't. But most weren't facing in the same direction anyway.

Now Lieutenant Norris spotted something new lurching through the shadows. Something from the back of the caves had followed the 8th Company men back towards his fire.

Several somethings.

Norris' heart pounded in his chest, he started hyperventilating, gulping down air in fear. He experienced a distinct slackening of the bladder. He readied himself to order the 8th to attack whatever unspeakable evil was stalking them. The somethings shuffled into the light.

The somethings were wearing leather shorts.

One was wrapped in a massive brass tuba.

Many of the ancient, skeletal newcomers sported long wispy beards which clung to their skulls. Almost all carried huge beer tankards. Norris spotted that one without a beard carried eight tankards, impressively clutching four in each hand. It looked like it had once been busty; causing the Lieutenant to muse that he really ought to look into German culture aside from all the warmongering. They seemed like nice corpses.

Reaching the conclusion that the German undead would cause them no harm Norris's mind turned once again to food. He was on the verge of collapse.

The captain's leg twitched at his feet.

He really was terribly hungry ...

***

"Yerrrry!" The British undead Captain hopped threateningly towards the snatch squad. A rifleman ran either side of him, a net held between them. The corpse went down, thrashing and struggling.

Two more Germans piled onto him.

The fifth and sixth squad members rushed past to ensure no more British were in the vicinity. Rounding a corner they came skidding to a halt. By the light of a blazing fire they could make out a bloodcurdling scene. A human form crouched before them gnawing a hunk of charred flesh. The hunk of flesh had toes. The toes wiggled.

The creature had spotted them. Its ravenous eyes gleamed with insanity. It slowly stood, lifting the squirming leg above its head. It grinned, raised its face to the air and screamed, "Charrrge!"

A wave of undead flooded round their leader.

***

Something was seriously wrong. Barnbeck could hear screams from the other side of the door. Undead don't scream. Nazis do though.

Fahrenkrog was livid. "The whole project has been jeopardised by a few idiotic soldiers messing with the subjects. If the Glorichen-Verstorbenen fails, I'll never be allowed back to the arctic circle to finish my work with the UFOs."

Barnbeck, Fahrenkrog and ten soldiers were crammed into the chamber. Fifty more waited, lining the corridor outside.

Barnbeck stared through the window of the door. Lots of things were moving through the ethereal mist inside.

Suddenly something lurched up in front of the portal.

With a fearful screech, Barnbeck leapt backwards, stumbling over the soldiers behind him.

A man's face was framed by the portal, his eyes wide with terror, his German uniform torn and bloody.

"For god's sake, get that man in here!"

The massive door was swung open and the soldier was dragged in.

The poor soldier had obviously been driven insane with the trauma of events he'd experienced since entering the catacombs. He spat and babbled and scratched.

In one hand he clutched a twitching human leg.

"Now yer buggered!"

The Captain's half-eaten leg kicked Barnbeck square in the face.

Norris grabbed Professor Fahrenkrog by the lapels and dragged him back out into the cave. On the way out he wedged the Captain's leg firmly between the huge vault door and its frame.

"After him!" Barnbeck yelled, tugging helplessly at the decomposing mess jamming the door open.

Uncertain, German troops spilled into the mist-filled cavern, stumbling and faltering, none willing to be the first to pursue the crazed British Lieutenant and his captive into the unknown.

Fahrenkrog could be heard screaming and pleading somewhere in the distance.

Something arced through the air, smashing just metres away from the line of terrified Nazis.

It was a tankard.

"Charrrge!"

***

Postscript:

There are currently at least three major fast food chains operating in the UK with substantial amounts of red in their logos. All play repetitive music all day long. One has a ninety-nine pence menu.

All major stores in Europe use red 'Sale' stickers to entice customers to purchase products they have no use for. Ninety-nine is by far the most common amount of pennies or cents required in transactions across Europe.

In 1983 The German singer, Nena, achieved number one in the German singles chart with the song 99 Luftballons (German for 99 balloons). The song was later released to the English speaking world, with similar success, as 99 Red Balloons. To date no negative behaviour has been associated with the song.

edited by Stephanie Ellis & S.G. Mulholland

Dead Punny
by Ross Baxter

Jim Dalby smiled to himself as he completed the final tweaks to the website. He made a last check of the content, feeling like a proud father about to send a genius child off to their first day at school.

"Doctor Punctilious," he read loudly to himself. "Creator of tailored tales, unique yarns and personalised puns. Let a professional comedian create humour exclusive to you, at a cost to suit most pockets! Ideal for speeches, conferences, and parties – a new gag for each occasion. Contact me for further details."

With a nod of satisfaction he pressed send, confident that this new venture would finally reverse his flagging fortunes. The launch of his website coincided with an advert in the Birmingham Evening Post; an approach he felt would cover all options. All he had to do now was to wait for the phone calls and emails to come flooding in, and he swiftly opened his inbox and stared at the blank screen.

The minutes slowly turned into hours and his optimism started to waver, his expected deluge evaporating into a trickle of despondency. He rose sullenly from the desk, but as he did so a mail suddenly flashed into the empty inbox. With a yelp he grabbed the mouse and hungrily clicked on the bold line, eager to read the contents.

"Are you satisfied with the size of your penis?" he read aloud, his voice bitter with disappointment. The irony of the spam email was not lost on him; the size of his penis was the only thing in life that actually did satisfy him.

The trip to the Unemployment Benefit Office served only to increase his despondency. If he failed to find work in the next month they would cut his benefit, something he simply could not afford. Warehouse work or bricklaying were not for him; Jim was a comedian, an entertainer not a labourer. He often contented himself with the thought that other artists had struggled and were even persecuted for their art, a thought which gave him some consolation. But consolation was nowhere near as good as money.

Jim took a printed ticket which showed his place in the queue and found a seat in the far corner of the drab office, away from the others waiting. He always arrived early so as to beat the crowds, but still the visit usually entailed a long wait. From the length of the queue he estimated he would be here at least twenty minutes, and found a discarded newspaper to pass the time. As he opened the battered tabloid he sensed somebody walking towards him and looked up to see a figure in a grey hooded top. The figure said nothing but took the seat next to him, even though there were rows of empty seats to choose from. He groaned inwardly, returning his gaze to the newspaper to avoid any form of contact with the stranger.

"Are you Doctor Punctilious, creator of tailored tales, unique yarns and personalised puns?" the stranger asked in a low voice.

"Err ...," Jim started in surprise, gawping at the hooded figure. "Yes."

"Good," said the stranger. "How is business?"

Jim stared at the man, unable to see much of the face under the hood in the poor light of the office. Normally he would have lied and said business was fantastic, but waiting in the queue in the Unemployment Benefit Office was a bit of a giveaway.

"It's starting to pick up," Jim replied guardedly.

"Are you still taking commissions?" asked the stranger, his low voice devoid of accent or inflection.

"I can always squeeze another in, as the actress said to the bishop," Jim quipped.

The stranger did not laugh or even smile.

"In that case I'd like to talk business," said the stranger. "I'm working on a book, and I need help with some sections of it."

"A book?" Jim asked. "Well, if you were a chicken you'd be writing a *buk buk buk*."

Again, the stranger's face remained straight. "Yes, a book on crime. It's nearly finished but I need a variety of humorous ways for some of the characters to die in it; something comical which fits in with the persona of each character."

"Well, you're talking to the right person," Jim said, starting to rise to the occasion. "As long as crime does pay, I'd be happy to help."

"Crime pays very well," the stranger answered evenly. "I will need one amusing scenario per week, based on a set of characteristics that I'll give you. For each sketch I will pay you one thousand pounds."

Jim's heart suddenly sank. The stranger was obviously winding him up, a ruse he certainly did not find droll. "I suppose that'll be a thousand pounds in monopoly money then?"

"As I said," the stranger continued, "crime does pay. I'm offering you one thousand pounds in cash for each piece which fits the theme."

"We're sat in an Unemployment Benefit Office not a gentleman's club," Jim challenged bitterly. "Where are you going to get that sort of money from?"

"I'm prepared to give you the first payment up front," said the stranger, reaching under the hooded top and bringing out a large brown envelope.

"Yeah, right!" Jim scoffed, annoyed at the stranger's insistence to continue with the ploy.

The stranger gently opened the envelope and turned it so that Jim could see the contents. Jim peered in and his mouth dropped open in surprise.

"Do you believe me now?" the stranger asked.

"Yes. Yes I do!" Jim gasped.

"Good. All you have to do is come up with a funny end for a small-time drug dealer who pushes weed from the back of his car. He targets young women mainly, using their addiction and his supply as a way of getting girlfriends," said the stranger. "Do you think you can come up with something?"

"Is the Pope a Catholic?" Jim shot back hungrily. "You bet I can come up with something! How do I get it to you?"

"Just type it up, and I'll collect it from you in a week's time."

Jim eyed the envelope with greed, expecting to hear the catch. Instead the stranger rose and left the envelope on the plastic seat. Without a word or a glance back he walked towards the sliding doors of the grim foyer and out into the rainy street beyond. Jim sat motionless, waiting for the hooded figure to reappear. He thought of the numerous shows on television which worked on the premise of trickery such as this, and glanced around to see where the grinning host would suddenly spring from. Seconds turned into minutes and he still sat alone with the envelope in front of him. He picked up the manila package and slipped his hand inside to caress the cash within. It felt real. Again he looked around, studying the dismal surroundings and the glum figures waiting in the queue. He then realised that the number on his ticket had already been passed, and that he had lost his place in the line. But instead of anger he smiled. He balled up the ticket and dropped it on the grimy floor, thinking his time had finally come. Gripping the envelope tightly he strode out of the room into the downpour outside, his mind overflowing with a deluge of ideas.

***

Coming up with a humorous ending for the small-time dealer had been easier than Jim had imagined. He actually came up with the lines on the walk home from the Unemployment Benefit Office, although he did polish it over the following days. The story revolved around the weed dealer getting stoned to death, and Jim had thrown in a number of other puns to the tale for good measure. It was the easiest money he had ever made, and the thought buoyed him up like never before, making him hungry for the week to pass and get the next assignment from the mysterious hooded stranger.

When Wednesday finally arrived he put on his new jacket and marched happily towards the Unemployment Benefit Office. Inside he scanned the same old faces for his new employer, but did not recognise him. Without taking a ticket he sat down to wait, the typed manuscript safely folded in his pocket. After a few minutes he became aware of a presence standing to his side and looked up to see a callow, humourless youth in a dirty grey jogging suit sporting a ostentatious gold-encrusted baseball cap.

"Hey, mate," said the youth. "Are you Doctor Punkt …, Punktil …, Punktellisus?"

"Doctor Punctilious," Jim corrected.

"Yeah," the youth nodded. "What you said."

"I am," replied Jim.

"I'm supposed to take an envelope from you, and give you this one," grunted the youth, pulling a crumpled manila envelope from the back of his soiled jogging bottoms.

Jim eyed the envelope with distaste, exchanging it for his pristine version containing the typed script. The youth nodded and swaggered towards the exit, putting on a pair of expensive-looking headphones on top of his oversized hat. Jim watched him leave before eying the creased envelope eagerly. Unable to wait until he got home he carefully tore open the envelope to peer inside. A thin wad of fifty-pound notes lay at the bottom. Without taking the money out he peeled each note off with his damp thumb and forefinger and counted twenty.

"Unbelievable!" he whispered.

With a wide smile he then withdrew the single sheet of white paper and silently read it to himself: *Thank you in anticipation of your finished work. Your next assignment is to write a humorous ending for a bank manager. Someone people look up to, but a person who abuses the trust and power his position bestows. When you have finished, email it to me at Falsename666@hotmail.co.uk. Your money and next assignment will come next week."*

Jim grinned, carefully folding the sheet and replacing it in the envelope, his mind filling with ideas as he strolled out of the drab office.

***

The following Wednesday, Jim sat down to breakfast and switched on the radio. The local news was running a story about a man found dead in his wrecked vehicle on an estate in the city. Police were baffled by the fact that the victim, a known local drug dealer, had apparently been stoned to death, with bricks and rubble covering the car and body. Jim listened with curiosity; interested in how close the circumstances were to the funny ending he had penned for the well-paying stranger. Except that it did not sound so funny when read out in a news bulletin.

A sudden knocking at the front door made him start. He listened puzzled; it was rare for him to get any visitors, never mind one this early in the morning. Tightening his dressing gown around him he cautiously made towards the door, opening it a crack to peer through.

"I've a document for the Doctor," announced a man in blue Fed-Ex overalls. "I need a signature."

Jim opened the door and accepted the slim package eagerly. The courier held out a terminal and Jim signed and printed his name on the pitted screen.

The Fed-Ex man frowned. "You've signed it as Jim Dalby. It's addressed to Doctor ... err ..."

"I'm Doctor Punctilious," Jim cut in. "It's a pseudonym."

The courier regarded him blankly.

"It's my stage name."

"Oh, a pseudonym. Is that some sort of octopus show?" the courier asked.

This time it was Jim's turn to stare back blankly. "No."

"Fine," the courier shrugged. "Thanks."

Jim quickly closed the door as the Fed-Ex man departed. Ripping the envelope open he was disappointed to find a single sheet of paper, and no money. He read the note swiftly: *Your email regarding the demise of the bank manager was received. You can collect your payment and next assignment only if you follow the instructions below exactly:*

    1.   *Get to the construction site for the new bypass at Gravelly Hill at exactly midnight tonight.*
    2.   *Go to the third bridge support – the money and assignment will be there.*

    Jim shook his head, annoyed at the unnecessary drama being introduced to their relationship. But given the amount of easy money offered he was more than happy to indulge his employer.

***

    The construction site was easy to find and, with the absence of any security, gaining access proved simple. Jim trudged through the sucking mud, his torch picking out his path between the puddles. Above him loomed the half-finished road bridge, sheathed by a lattice of scaffolding, canvas and formwork. He counted the new supports which rose from the churned sludge, fresh concrete drying in a jacket of wooden props.

    The third support seemed the newest, and moonlight glistened off the still-damp concrete seeping through the joins in the wooden mould casing. Jim peered at the column, looking for his promised payment and next assignment. He picked his way carefully around the support, sidestepping the muddy puddles and debris-strewn floor. At the other side one of the planks appeared loose, hanging off the concrete interior by just a tattered strap at the bottom. It was the only place which could hide anything on the construct, and Jim moved closer to inspect the errant timber. There was definitely something there, something protruding from the inner grey surface. Jim shone his torch in to get a closer look.

    "Shit!" he yelped, stepping backwards and dropping the torch.

    He stared in shock, seeing the unmistakable shape of a hand in the moonlight. The hand seemed to be part submerged in the concrete column, its grey crusted fingers gripping a small package. Cursing silently he shook his head, unable to see the funny side of the elaborate joke. He leaned forward to get a closer look, fascinated by the detail of the dummy hand. Matted hairs on the digits, broken nails and even a wedding ring; it looked almost real. Too real. In a cold sweat Jim slowly reached forward to retrieve the package clutched by the hand, watching in horror as the dead fingers stiffly parted when he pulled it free. Jim knew it was no dummy hand. It was the hand of a dead bank manager whose fate Jim had penned a week earlier: *Buried alive in concrete at an urban building site so that he could become a pillar of his community.*

Jim turned and ran.

***

The money lay on the table in front of him. It had been there for three days now, untouched since he had counted it. Jim once more sat at the table and stared at the notes, still wrestling with the decision he had to make. He had written two humorous endings as instructed, and was three thousand pounds better off. But both endings seemed to have come true; the stoned drug dealer and pillar-of-the-community bank manager. The next assignment was printed on the plain white sheet contained in the package, an ending for a local politician who had lied her way to the top through broken promises and made-up stories. Initially he had tried to discover who the victim would be, but quickly realised that lying and breaking promises seemed to be a common trait for most politicians.

Jim knew he had a duty to go to the police. He also knew such a course of actions would result not only in his source of future money drying up, but he would probably also have to give back the money he had earned so far. It was the worst dilemma of his life.

The third ending had been completed earlier, and sat already attached to the new email address contained in the instruction. Coming up with the ending had been as simple as the first two, this demise involving the politician ending up literally full of shit. Jim looked hungrily at the send icon on his laptop, his mind debating what the right thing to do was. Then he decided, and clicked on send.

***

The next few days passed quickly; the decision to send the politician's demise to the stranger had not troubled him as much as he thought it would. He concluded that this was something to do with how society viewed politicians, something he had certainly experienced first-hand from the time he spent at the Unemployment Benefit Office. He also countered that it was not he doing the killing, his mind harking back to Oscar Wilde's quote of *'Life imitates art far more than art imitates Life'*. Even so he still felt uneasy, nervously waiting for the next package of instructions and money.

He did not have to wait long. This time he received an anonymous email, directing him to attend an open-air rock concert the coming weekend where he could collect the next package. Jim relaxed slightly, knowing there would be little danger of a killing taking place or discovering a corpse amidst the huge crowd of people attending. The line-up of bands was also fairly good, and he actually began to look forward to attending the event.

When Saturday finally arrived he donned his festival gear and caught the bus to the venue. Not knowing where to go he wandered around the many stages and stalls, drinking in the atmosphere and sampling the bands. As he queued at a burger stand a vibration from his phone signalled a text telling him to go to the thirteenth cubicle in a row of portable toilets near the main stage. Jim's heart sank, and glumly he left the queue and trudged towards the battered row of blue plastic conveniences.

The thirteenth cubicle appeared locked, a red circle surrounding the grimy door handle. Jim gingerly tried the door anyway and was not surprised when it opened. His surprise came when he looked inside to find the floor removed, and in the recess below lay a body. The outlet pipes from the cubicles converged in a pit below the missing floor, a torrent of filth pouring over the prostrate corpse which floated open-mouthed. Jim could not recognise the cadaver but guessed it was a politician, now literally full of shit. Tearing his eyes from the gruesome sight he saw a small parcel taped to the empty toilet paper dispenser. Holding his breath, he stepped forward onto the ledge in the cubicle to reach the packet but his weight caused the ledge to suddenly give way and he tumbled down into the pit below. As he floundered in the sucking sewage the band on stage finished their cover of Dire Straits' *Money for Nothing* and launched into Eurythmics *Here comes that Sinking Feeling*.

Disappearing from view, Doctor Punctilious completely missed the pun.

The Woman in Slacks
by Stephanie Ellis

It had been one of those grim, dreary days when Vincent had first seen her. His train had eventually pulled into the station some three hours after it was supposed to and he was tired, hungry and extremely irritable - in other words a typical day's commute although one had sent him to some godforsaken little town on the Norfolk coast. Despite arrangements having been made, there was no one to meet him and the taxi ranks were empty. In the background a church clock struck twelve. He'd been warned about the witching hour before he'd set off. "Pray you get there before twelve," old Mr Tomlinson had said. Once it strikes the hour, you're on your own.

He'd been right.

As Vincent dragged his suitcase down the high street, 'Open' signs turned over before his eyes. People vanished in front of him. Soon it was just him, his luggage - and her.

She was stood in the archway beneath the old town hall that dominated the market place. It was the slightest of movements that had brought her to his attention. He could not make out her features from this distance but he could clearly see her trousers, coloured in the most gruesome shade of brown known to man. It was with an uneasy feeling of dread that he approached this solitary figure. Closing in on her he noticed that the trouser fabric seemed to shine, even on such an overcast day as this. He shuddered at the cheap polyester, his sensibilities revolted by this curse of mankind. Still, he had no choice.

"Excuse me," he called as she moved away. "Excuse me, could you ..."

She was gone. Bewildered, Vincent gazed around. There were no doors or alleyways down which she could have gone. She had simply vanished into thin air. Across the road an old pub caught his eye, its bowed walls and black timbers hinting at extreme antiquity. The King's Head seemed to be the only establishment that was still open. Wearily Vincent walked through its doors, ducking the low beams that supported a ceiling bowed with age and looking as though it might split apart at any minute. So concerned was he with the possible danger overhead, he paid little attention to the floor worn uneven by generations which caused him to stumble as if already drunk. By the time he reached the small dining area and had settled himself at a window seat, he was feeling more than a touch unbalanced. He took out his phone to make a call to the Brewers to explain his late arrival. There was no signal. With a sigh he returned his phone to his pocket.

"Won't get no signal round 'ere," said a gruff voice behind him. Vincent turned round. A grizzled old man sat by the open fire. "Signal always goes when it rains, which is most days. Not keen on the sun much neither, and if she's walking... well then you don't stand a cat's chance." With that he turned his back on Vincent and resumed his contemplation of the fire.

Slightly nonplussed, Vincent shrugged and picked up the menu.

"Course you could always go to the park and stand on the bench by the duck pond - third one along as you go into the park from the high street. Usually a queue this time of day though, what with it bein' early closin' an' all."

Vincent turned round again. The old man had disappeared.

"Don't worry about old Jack," said a waitress materialising at his elbow. "He's harmless enough, a regular walking encyclopaedia of local information. He's probably gone to join the queue."

"Why doesn't he just use the pay phone here?" Vincent indicated a phone on the wall near the bar.

"And let everyone know your business?" she said grimly, her voice betraying the tone of one who spoke from personal experience. "He wants his privacy."

She took his order and left him to ponder the dynamics of the small town mentality. Vincent couldn't imagine how standing on a park bench bellowing into a phone with half the town listening in was any more private than making a call in a more-or-less deserted bar.

The waitress returned with a surprisingly generous plate of steak and chips. He remembered to ask for the receipt. If he had to come to such a place as this then he was determined to get as much as he could out of his expenses.

"That man, Jack," he said as he took the proffered ticket and slipped into his wallet. "He said you couldn't get a signal if she's walking. What did he mean by that?"

The waitress, Emily, according to her name badge, visibly paled and glanced around nervously. The landlord was watching her carefully. "Oh nothing, nothing. That's just Jack as I said. He can be a silly old fool."

"Yes, but ... she?" he prompted.

"I'm sorry. I've got to get back to the kitchen. Can't stand here chatting during the lunchtime rush," and with a quick apologetic smile, she was gone.

Vincent gazed blankly around the empty bar. If there was a rush it had certainly passed him by. He leaned back in his chair. A full stomach, comfortable surroundings, it made up in some small part for the dreadful journey. He sipped his pint slowly and surveyed the view from the window. The streets were still deserted but in the shadow of the archway he saw her again, the unmistakeable sheen of those dreadful trousers drawing his eye in, hypnotizing him.

"Sir, sir. Are you alright?"

Vincent jumped. The landlord was looking anxiously down at him.

"Huh?"

"You were looking a little peaky sir. I was just wondering if you were alright?" There was a concerned look on the man's face but Vincent wasn't sure whether it was for himself or for his business as the landlord's nervous eyes kept flicking towards the door.

"Yes, yes, I'm fine," said Vincent hastily. "Thank you for your concern though."

"Well you can't be too careful nowadays. Only last week we had a customer - a man about the same age as you - sat here gazing out the window, like you, and when I came over - well, he was dead like. Had a heart attack. Frightened the life out of me I can tell you."

"I'm sure it must've been quite a shock," said Vincent slightly disturbed by the conversation.

"It was at that," agreed the landlord, nodding his head emphatically. "Got me and my staff onto First Aid courses pretty sharpish, I can tell you." The landlord waved his arm at the wall behind the bar where a range of First Aid certificates were proudly displayed.

"That's very ... reassuring," said Vincent, slightly at a loss for words. Time for a change of subject he felt. "Tell me. There's a woman I've seen in the street, a couple of times now. Seems a bit ... odd. She's out there now, under the arch. I was wondering if you knew who she was?"

The landlord peered out of the window. "No one there now I'm afraid. What did she look like?"

Vincent shrugged his shoulders. "Don't know really, I couldn't quite catch her face, but her trousers ... they were truly terrible."

Like the waitress, the landlord's face had gone white. "Can't help you there I'm afraid. I'd better get back to the bar, things to do. A pub doesn't run itself you know." Then he was gone.

Vincent glanced at his watch. The afternoon was drawing on, time for him to get moving. "Brown trousers" would have to wait. A local taxi firm had stuck their card above the phone in the bar. Vincent called a cab. The landlord watched him silently as he left.

"Where to guv'nor?"

"Lych House, do you know it?"

"Oh, the Brewer's old place do you mean? Yes I know it. Lucky you called me now. Any later and the tide would be in and you wouldn't have been able to get out there today."

"Tide?"

"Didn't you know? There's been a lot of erosion in these parts. Lych House is gradually getting cut off."

The sky hung heavy with rain, black clouds pressed down on the bleak landscape as the taxi sped through it. Puddles became deeper and wider in the rutted roads but the driver didn't slow down. It was as if he wanted to get the job done and over with as quickly as possible.

"Do you want me to wait?" asked the cabbie when they finally arrived.

"No, no. I've arranged to stay over for the night."

"You're ... staying ... over?"

"Yes. The family want me to go through some old papers. They said I'd have everything I needed to be comfortable."

"I hope they included some holy water and a wooden stake in that," said the taxi driver.

"Pardon?"

"Nothing, nothing. Just my little joke." The cabbie avoided his eyes. "I'll come over tomorrow morning to take you back."

"Don't worry about that. I'll give you a call when I need you."

"You'll be lucky," said the taxi driver. "No phone in the house and no signal either."

"Ah. Alright then. I'll um ... see you in the morning."

The taxi drove off leaving Vincent to take in the full grimness of Lych House. It was certainly an imposing building but it had most definitely seen better days. Rotting window frames barely contained the glass which visibly moved in the howling wind. The door didn't seem in much better condition either and the brickwork was beginning to crumble away. He found the key he'd been given and turned the lock. The door groaned in protest, grudgingly allowing him in. It smelled damp and musty. If it hadn't been raining he would have flung open the windows. Vincent left his case in the hall and examined his new surroundings.

The rooms seemed barely habitable with peeling wallpaper and noticeable splodges of mould on the ceilings.

One small room, obviously a study, was in slightly better condition. A fire had been laid ready in the hearth, matches placed by a storm lamp on the coffee table. A comfortable looking camp bed had been made up. His host's thoughtfulness had extended to a kettle and the necessities to make a hot drink. A cool box contained milk and beer.

An envelope had been placed on his pillow. It contained a welcome from his clients. They hoped he would find everything he needed in the study. A hot meal could be had using the microwave they'd left him for the purpose. Vincent glanced around. It was sat, rather incongruously, on the Victorian sideboard. Some ready meals had been buried beneath the beer. Amongst the general instructions was a strange warning - on no account was he to go upstairs during the hours of darkness, no matter what he heard - or thought he heard.

Vincent went over to the grimy window and cleared a hole in the dirt. It was still dark from the rain clouds but night had not yet fallen.

Curiosity piqued, Vincent went upstairs.

There were three bedrooms, all empty of furniture, a rather disgustingly-stained bathroom and a small room at the end of the corridor which, from the fading border of fluffy bunnies, had once been a nursery. The only item in there was a rocking chair. He shrugged his shoulders and went back downstairs. It had suddenly occurred to him that a toilet was a necessity. What if he should need one in the night? Returning to the study, he re-examined the letter. At the bottom of the page he noticed a small PTO. He flipped it over. Toilet facilities can be found outside. Outside? He stuck his head out the back door. Unceremoniously positioned in the middle of the yard amongst a pile of building material was a portaloo. Someone had also thoughtfully hung a key and toilet roll by the kitchen door.

Vincent didn't fancy the idea of such a night trip - perhaps a bucket could be found.

Back in the study once more, he unpacked his belongings, slipped his pyjamas under the pillows, and hoped it wouldn't be too long before he was able to slip between the sheets. Then he lit the fire, brewed a cup of tea and started to work his way through the boxes of papers that had been left out for him. There was nothing exciting there, dry legal documents, barely legible land deeds. It all had to be catalogued and sorted. He was thinking about taking a break when he pulled out a pile of old letters, these were personal correspondence.

Dear Rosemary, began the first one. *I am sorry to have to say goodbye to you like this but I couldn't think of any other way. You really are a lovely girl and I'm sure one day you'll find the right man, I'm afraid that it's just not meant to be me,*
Yours Affectionately, Roger
PS. You really should ditch those trousers that you're always in. I mean, polyester, and THAT colour. Really darling!

Vincent thought of the woman under the arch. He picked up another letter.

Dear Rosemary, I'm sorry to have to ...

It was almost identical to the first except that this was signed Geoffrey and he too delivered a parting shot at the trousers, this time complaining of the static shocks he received when close to her. Didn't she realise they could seriously damage a man's chances of becoming a father?

The next letter was from a Jack. Vincent wondered if he was the same one that he had met in the pub. Somehow he found it hard to picture him as the courting kind. Perhaps when he was younger. Vincent checked the date, it was thirty-odd years ago. That made it a bit more feasible. He too complained about the trousers. Beneath the letters was a small diary.

14th Feb. Valentine's Day. No roses or chocolates for me. Just a cowardly letter from Roger finishing with me. He even had the nerve to criticise the clothes I wear. Polyester is so easy to wash. Bet he has someone to do the laundry for him.

The next entry was a month letter and recorded her response to Geoffrey's missive and then after another month there was a reference to Jack's letter. And so it went on. Many more entries detailing her breakups - she must've worked her way through half the town's male population he thought - before it finished on a final one.

31st October. The whole town's laughing at me. They think I don't see them but I do, sniggering behind their lace curtains, making sarcastic remarks about elasticated waistbands. If only they'd try them themselves I'm sure they'd change their minds, I mean I've got plenty of spares. It was a lucky day when that Transylvanian cargo vessel broke up on the coast and they all washed up. And that strange sailor was a real gentleman. There was no need to tell the authorities about him was there? He just needed a bit of time to recover before he set off to sea again. And he'd been no bother, no bother at all. In fact I never saw him during the day. He kept himself to himself. Like I said ... a real gentleman. Not like the others, they need to be taught a lesson ...

Vincent rubbed his eyes. This was all such a long time ago, and yet ... he glanced at the clock. It was ten already. Where had the time gone? Time to try the facilities. Wearily he hauled himself out of his seat and headed out into the yard. Thankfully the earlier storm seemed to have eased somewhat. He entered the plastic cubicle and sat down. There was a loud rumble from somewhere and then the ground began to shake. He grabbed at the side of the cubicle to steady himself but still the growling continued. It was as if pressure from something deep below was building up and getting ready to explode. He tried to stand only to tangle himself up in his trousers as he did so, they remained resolutely around his ankles. The portaloo started to rock from side to side. Maybe it was kids, it was nearly Halloween after all.

"Hey!" he cried. "Pack it in." There was only a shrill laugh in reply and the toilet continued to move. Any minute now he thought and it would go over and then he'd really be in the...

The cubicle slammed down, the door flying open as it did so, spewing Vincent and its more unsavoury contents out into the night. The rumbling stopped and silence rolled over the house again. Trembling, he bent down to pull his trousers up only to jerk his hand away in disgust. Whatever they were covered in he didn't want to know and gingerly stepped out of the offending garment.

He left them lying there by the prone cubicle. A bucket. Next time he would definitely use a bucket.

He quickly made his way back to the kitchen, washing himself down as best he could at the sink. As he dried himself he noticed something hanging over the back of a chair. It was a pair of brown, polyester trousers, complete with elasticated waist. No chance he thought. Lucky I brought spares with me. He turned his back on the trousers and returned to the study, the smell from his recent mishap clinging to him as he went. Miserably he searched for his deodorant, debating how strongly he could afford to spray the aerosol without bringing on an asthma attack. Half-an-hour later, he was able to put his inhaler down and sit by the fire, enjoying its warmth. It was a good time to indulge in some of that whisky his clients had so kindly left him he thought and swiftly knocked back a glass. What had happened? A freak storm, that was all, which just so happened to have rather bizarre consequences. Logical, it was all perfectly logical. And the trousers in the kitchen? They must've been there earlier, he just hadn't seen them.

He poured himself another glass and leaned back in his chair. He would just sit quietly for a while and then ...

Crash! Vincent jumped up so quickly that he knocked the whisky bottle over. He watched in horror as an unfortunate wet patch spread across his trousers. With a sigh he stepped out of the clothing and draped it over the side of a chair. They would soon be dry. True, they'd smell like a brewery tomorrow but that was a million times better than the garment he'd abandoned outside. He still had another pair of jeans as well as some pyjamas. There was a dull thud outside the door and the lamplight flickered alarmingly. Vincent moved towards the door and slowly turned the handle. He held up the lantern to illuminate the corridor but could see nothing, only a never-ending darkness. At his feet was a small mound. Slowly he bent down to examine the object. Trousers. Again. And these most certainly had not been there earlier. He stepped back quickly and slammed the door shut. He could see no bolt or lock and so dragged a chair over and propped it beneath the handle.

The letter had told him not to go upstairs and despite hearing rather sulky footsteps stomping overhead, Vincent thought that was fine by him. He could never understand those horror films where the characters went off into the darkness to investigate strange happenings. They always died, or became possessed, or both. He had no intention of succumbing to such stupidity. He would stay here, in the study, and not go anywhere until it was light. But first he'd put on some trousers. It was going to be bad enough if he did end up running screaming from the house but if he did that and wasn't wearing any trousers, oh the humiliation.

As if on cue the window blew open. A huge gust of wind sent his papers whirling, clothes spinning. Something brown blasted in through the window, heading straight for him. He ducked at the last minute and whatever it was went straight into the fire causing it to hiss and spit. Vincent ran across to the window to secure it once more and pulled the curtains to, shutting out the night. Returning to the fireplace, a small fragment of smoking material fluttered onto the hearthstone. He could make out the words 100% polyester.

Vincent backed away, stumbling over his suitcase and landing on the camp bed. He pulled out a pair of jeans, disturbing his pyjamas as he did so. Hadn't he placed them under the pillow earlier? He could've sworn he had. Carefully he lifted up the pillow. There, where his pyjamas should've been, was yet another pair of those bloody trousers.

Perhaps it was time to get drunk, being haunted by a ghost with a brown polyester trouser fetish was pretty disturbing and not easy to cope with when sober. What had the taxi driver said? He hoped I'd brought some holy water and a stake.

Well he didn't have that, but there was a bible on the bookcase, he'd got a crucifix - admittedly he'd bought it for Susan, his sister so it was a bit girlie - but she wouldn't mind if he wore it in the meantime. Besides, the way she dabbled in religion, she'd have probably converted to Buddhism by the time he saw her again and the cross wouldn't be appropriate any more.

He grabbed the book, slipped the necklace over his head and dragged the armchair over so that its back was against the wall. Nothing would be able to creep up behind him. Then both the lamp and the fire went out. Somewhere in the house a clock struck midnight, yet the clocks he'd seen earlier had all stopped.

"This is not happening, this is not happening," he moaned, repeating the mantra over and over again. Now something was pulling at his legs, tugging at his jeans. He swatted the unseen hands away with the bible. There was a howl in the darkness and his invisible attacker backed off but the respite was only temporary. Back came his assailant, this time grappling with his belt, his fly buttons, desperately trying to tear his trousers off him. It was a nightmare parody of some much more enjoyable evenings. He tried not to think of what it might lead to.

"No," he shouted. "No! Don't you understand that when a man says no, he means no?"

Silence. Somehow he managed to dress himself again whilst retaining a firm grip on his bible. Whatever was attacking him didn't like that book and he was damned if he was going to let his one weapon go. He fished out his crucifix and pointed it into the darkness. "Begone foul fiend," he cried, trying to ignore how ridiculous he sounded.

There was a mocking laugh. His attacker didn't think too much of his effort either and then both lamp and fire flickered back to life. He glanced at his watch. It was one o'clock. How many hours to dawn? Three? Four? It was going to be a long night. Regretfully he pushed the beer away. He needed to stay sober and awake. Coffee.

By the time daylight had begun to seep through the curtain, he was a nervous wreck. His heart was pounding from the caffeine hit it had taken and his legs were twitching and jerking manically. He got up and walked around the room again. The fire was out. It had been smothered by a delivery of trousers somewhere between the hours of two and three. He preferred to remain cold rather than go near those garments. It was a sleeping monster, any minute now they would launch a four-pair attack. His hand cramped. He had not let go of the bible once. It was getting light, surely he would be able to put it down now so that he could massage a bit of life back into his fingers and he was still wearing his crucifix after all.

Very slowly, he put the book on the table, keeping his eye fixed on the dead fire all the time. As he wriggled his fingers, he felt himself start to tingle. At first he ignored the feeling, it was just his circulation re-establishing itself. Then the tingling became a prickling. He glanced in the mirror and was shocked to see that his hair was standing out in all directions, just like that experiment everybody did at school with a Van der Graaf generator.

The chair under the door handle toppled forward and the door banged open. He grabbed the bible once more and stepped out into the hallway. The air felt as if it were alive with static. He had to get out of the house but which way? Memories of the portaloo incident returned, that ruled out the back door.

He took a deep breath and ran for it, chanting the only prayer he knew - which happened to be from the funeral service, he had been to rather a lot of funerals lately. It wasn't very comforting but still it was better than nothing he thought. "Ashes to ashes, dust to dust," he intoned. He was at the front door. *'Don't look back, don't look back,'* he told himself. He looked back.

All the way up the stairs and beyond, as far as the eye could see were pairs of brown polyester trousers. There was a low humming sound, it almost sounded like ... no, it couldn't be ... yes *'100% polyester, elasticated waist, comfort fit, 100% polyester, elasticated waist, comfort fit,'*.

He knew now who was haunting him. The voice, Rosemary's voice, cooed softly at first. A temptress's voice that became more strident, more vicious, as he refused to yield to the advances of her gifts, rejected her suit. The words, her mantra, were repeated again and again in an hypnotic rhythm that threatened to transfix him forever. But then he saw the trousers and terror took hold. And nothing could stop him.

Vincent flung himself at the door but the rain-warped wood prevented his escape, held the door fast. Behind him he could hear the mass move, creeping down the stairs, coming to claim him. Any minute now his attacker would be trying to pull his jeans off again. He gave another tug and the door gave way once and for all. He sprinted out into the morning air and freedom. The mist disoriented him briefly, the sea attacking the grounds of Lych House in a pincer movement from either side. He sought out the trees that stood guardian to the low-lying land, marking the path back to solid ground and reality.

The tide hadn't gone completely out but it was shallow enough for him to run through. He kept on, even though his heart was hammering and his lungs felt as if they were about to burst. Finally, when he thought he could run no longer, he saw a car coming towards him. It was the taxi-driver. Vincent flagged him down and jumped in.

"My god mate, you alright? You look as though you've seen a ghost."

"Yeah," he replied breathlessly. "I think you could say that."

The cabbie looked at him thoughtfully. "You know you should really get out of those wet things as quickly as possible.

Hang on a tick, I think I've got something in the boot that'll just do the trick."

The taxi-driver got out of the car and rifled around in the boot for a minute before reappearing.

"Here you go mate. 100% polyester, elasticated waist, comfort fit." The cabbie's eyes had glazed over.

Vincent started to tingle again. His hands fumbled uselessly with the seatbelt. The taxi-driver had started the engine but he wasn't going back to town. Instead he was heading for Lych House. The cabbie looked in the mirror and smiled at him. "She's waiting for you, you know. She's been waiting a long, long time for you."

"Who?"

"Who? Why the woman in slacks of course."

Vincent felt his belt start to unravel. Slowly his fly buttons popped open and then his jeans were tugged fiercely off. The window opened and his denims were tossed outside with a triumphant laugh. The brown trousers were reverently pulled over Vincent's shaking legs, up around his waist.

"100% polyester, elasticated waist, comfort fit," he murmured, smiling happily as he stood once more at the door to Lych House. A woman's hand reached out and took his.

"Ah Vincent. I'm so glad you've come back. And I must say you look divine in those trousers. They really are to die for."

Vincent allowed himself to be led back inside.

Those who subsequently saw him on the few occasions before he disappeared completely commented on his attire. "You know he never wears anything but those awful brown trousers? Even tried to get me to wear them, slipped a pair in my briefcase but I dumped them pretty sharpish. Wouldn't be seen dead ..."

Joseph Tomlinson sighed as he watched the train depart. He could think of far better things than tracking down an AWOL employee of his father's but Vincent's sister had said she would be very grateful, *very* grateful. He made his way across the market place towards The King's Head. He didn't notice the woman hidden in the shadows of the old town hall.

edited by Stephanie Ellis & S.G. Mulholland

Tie Bride
by T.M. McLean

Trevor could not get used to the smell. One moment his nostrils were filled with the pleasing aroma of chicken being grilled by one of the many street vendors, the next he was assaulted by the rank stench of pure sewage. It did not make for a pleasant combination. But that was just the way things were in Bangkok.

Mixed in with the smells were the people. The men looked mostly like cutthroats, sour expressions plastered onto their scarred faces. Many of them were holding signs detailing the various different types of shows available in the bars. The women were a truly mixed bag. Some of them had the appearance of super models: long legs, high heels and short dresses. Others looked like hags who had somehow managed to escape the clutches of the devil in order to sell miniature Buddha statues from market stalls. All around people could be heard haggling, car horns beeped and salesmen shouted. It seemed like chaos, but, somehow, it all fell into place, creating a vibrancy Trevor had never experienced.

Trevor paused by one of the stalls to check out the trinkets. It did not shock him to see sex toys for sale beside the selection of carved animals and Buddhist souvenirs. Children, both local and tourist, were happily rummaging through the wares beside him until a white woman, German from the sounds of her, slapped her daughter's hand away from an uncomfortably large looking dildo and grabbed her by the arm, before swiftly dragging her away into the press of the crowd. Trevor chuckled to himself.

"You want to buy?" asked the stall owner as she thrust the masturbation aid at Trevor. "Good for wife. She enjoy very much when she alone at home."

"No thanks. I don't have a wife," Trevor told her.

"Ah, no wife, no matter. I have for you," she twisted around and reached for something behind her. "Look, for you!" It was an inflatable doll, which, according to the packaging, had three entry points. Trevor laughed again. He thought about buying it to use later, but instead he held one of his palms out in front of him and shook his head before moving on. There would be better opportunities, he wouldn't have to resort getting his end away with a rubber woman just yet. The night was still young. *This place is insane*, he thought, and he loved every minute of it.

Walking on, he was stopped by one of the men with a sign. "Cheap show," he said to Trevor, using his free hand to indicate the different delights on offer.

Trevor looked it over. "What do you recommend?"

"Many good shows. Cheap. We got Cigarette Show, Naked Dance Show, Banana Show, and Ping Pong show . . . many good, cheap shows for you."

"I'm not interested in that," Trevor said. He'd already seen a Ping Pong show when he was in Benidorm earlier that year. "I'm looking for some real action. Know what I mean?"

It had been a while since Trevor had really enjoyed himself, although he had managed to get a couple of thrills while he was in Singapore. People criticised the transport system there for being too crowded, but that was exactly how Trevor liked it. For him the tight press of people on the MRT was like heaven. He enjoyed nothing more than rubbing himself against an unsuspecting passenger. Female passengers only, though. The motion of the train gave him the perfect cover for thrusting back and forth against an oriental beauty's buttocks. Sometimes they noticed, sometimes they didn't. It was far more enjoyable when they did. They loved it too, Trevor was sure of that, despite them pulling shocked faces when they saw his bulge. One foxy little minx had even reached behind her and put her hand around it. Maybe she thought it was a part of someone's bag or something. She didn't think that after he twitched it a couple of times. She gasped and moved to another part of the train, but she had kept her eyes on him for the rest of the journey. *She wants it*, Trevor had thought at the time, *they all do*.

"Of course, of course," the man's face contorted into something that was probably meant to be a smile but looked more like a grimace. "You want private one on one action with sweet Thai lady?"

The man put his sign down so that it rested against his leg. He made an O shape with the thumb and index finger of his left hand and used his right index finger to poke in and out of the hole.

Trevor told him that that was exactly what he wanted. Ever since Maureen, Trevor's girlfriend, had decided to leave Bangkok early to return to her friend in Singapore, he had been eager to try out Thailand's legendary hospitality. He was glad to be on his own, Maureen was a complete dullard. They had been together in Thailand for three days and all she wanted to do was visit one temple after another. Trevor hadn't minded at first, the temples attracted large crowds of tourists and the ruins of Ayutthaya had actually been a pretty impressive sight, but what he really wanted was to experience the Thailand his friends had told him about: the drinking, the parties and the girls. None of that was possible with Maureen hanging on his arm the whole time.

"It's not so cheap," Grimacer told him. "But I know who will help you out." He winked at Trevor and then babbled in his own language to another man beside him. He gave the man his sign and motioned for Trevor to follow him.

Together they walked through the crowded street. Trevor had to squeeze through the smallest gaps, making sure to brush his crotch against as many women as possible. They were mostly oblivious, despite his throbbing erection. Those that did notice were clearly used to being 'banged' into on the crowded streets and didn't even flinch, to Trevor's disappointment.

Even though it was very late, the Skytrain rumbled past overhead. Trevor decided that he would travel on it in the morning. The rush hour commuters would provide him with some early morning entertainment.

For a moment Trevor wondered if the man leading him was out to rob him, none of the locals could be trusted, but he didn't think so. He flexed his chest muscles the next time the man looked at him, making his tight T-shirt bounce and ensuring Grimacer knew not to try anything. Trevor outweighed most of the Thai people by at least four stone. Not only was he over six feet tall, but his four-hours-a-day gym muscles would make him an unlikely target.

"You are American?" Grimacer asked him, although it sounded more like a statement than a question.

"English," Trevor corrected him.

"Ah, London, God save the Queen." The man glanced at Trevor as they walked, another grotesque smile spreading across his face.

"Not London, mate. Manchester."

"Football, Alex Ferguson, Red Devils." The man was starting to get annoying.

"How far is it to the girls, mate?"

The smile disappeared from the man's face, replaced by a look of disappointment. "Not far," he said. "This way."

He led Trevor into an alleyway. Bags of rubbish had been left on the pavement and rats scurried amongst them, looking for morsels. A woman with a microphone came stumbling along the alley, the hellish, high-pitched sound of her singing echoed off the walls from a small speaker strapped to her chest. "What's her problem?" Trevor asked.

"She's blind, cannot see, and now she's singing for the money."

Well, there was no way she would get any from Trevor. *Even the people are like rats here*, he thought, *filthy cockroaches*.

They walked down the scruffy alley for some time, the noise from the main street faded, except for the occasional beep from the traffic. It didn't look to Trevor as though they were on their way to the sort of high class establishment he had been imagining. He wondered again if this man could be trusted. *What if he's leading me to some gangster hideout?*

"Listen, pal," Trevor said. "I think I'll just head back to the hotel. It's getting a bit late." The last thing he wanted was to be set upon by a dozen Thai boxing cutthroats. He felt that he could easily fight off one or two, but if they made a concerted effort then even he would have to yield.

"What? No need for that," the man told him. "We're almost there, just a little further."

Trevor decided to give the guy a chance. He didn't want to appear frightened. Just around a slight bend in the alley they came to a door, which matched the filth of their surroundings. The buildings were old, dark and oppressive. The narrow alleyway was completely deserted but the stifling night time heat made it feel crowded. The sewage smell persisted, just as it had around the market stalls.

Grimacer creaked the door open for Trevor, the sudden sound an alien screech in silence. "In there," he said.

It was dark inside, so Trevor stepped closer to look in. Stairs led upwards, just beyond the threshold, and he could hear music coming from the top. "Up there?" Trevor asked the man. "Are you coming?"

"No. You go up, alone. I go back to street."

He felt uneasy about entering the building by himself, but Trevor decided that it was worth the risk. If someone attacked him at the top he would just hit whoever it was as hard as he could and run back to the relative safety of the main street. Trevor nodded at the man and started walking into the doorway. There was a tap on his shoulder and, when Trevor turned, he saw the man's crooked grin and an outstretched hand. "Fifty baht," he said.

Reluctantly, Trevor took the money from his pocket and handed it to him. It seemed a little expensive for such a short journey. "There you go, mate."

"Thank you, my friend. Enjoy sweet Thai lady." Grimacer put his hands together in a praying gesture and bowed a few times. Trevor wasn't sure how long he kept that up because he turned to walk up the steps.

Excitement replaced apprehension as he began his ascent. The sewage smell from outside was substituted for the sweet scent of lavender, which grew stronger the higher he went. The music sounded peculiar to Trevor, some sort of xylophone or glockenspiel, he reckoned. He went around a corner at the top of the stairs and was delighted by what he saw.

Just as he had thought, a band was perched on a small stage in the corner of the room, playing xylophones. One of them had some kind of harp. Tables were set out like a restaurant and scantily clad dancing girls were entertaining the patrons as they drank and ate. Persian style artwork decorated the walls, and Trevor was relieved to see that he wasn't the only European in the room. A cluster of young white men were laughing and joking around, encouraging a group of Thai girls as they gyrated for their amusement. Trevor smiled as he ogled them.

"Good evening, sir. Do you like what you see?"

Trevor turned to his left and saw a stout Middle-Eastern man beside him. He was almost as tall as Trevor and around the same weight, but where Trevor rippled with muscles, this man hung soft and flabby with fat. He wondered how he hadn't noticed him before. "I like it a lot," Trevor told him.

"Welcome to Mahmoud's Palace, sir," said the man. His grin showed a gold tooth in an otherwise perfect set of teeth. "I am Mahmoud, prince of this establishment." His English was perfect, if it had not been for his dark complexion and oversized hooked nose, Trevor would have believed he was talking to a member of the English aristocracy.

"Thanks," said Trevor. "It's good to be here, although it was a little tricky to find."

"Alas, it is a necessity, sir. Unfortunately our line of business is not entirely legal, but we're tolerated by the authorities and business is good. Come, take a seat, have a drink and we will accommodate your needs."

Trevor was seated on a comfortable sofa, a small coffee table was set in front of it and a real beauty of a girl placed a glass of beer onto it for him. Mahmoud sat himself on an identical sofa opposite, clapped his hands twice and two more Thai girls wandered over, delightfully swaying their hips with every step. Mahmoud smiled as they positioned themselves around Trevor. One of them, the smallest, sat beside Trevor and rested her head against his shoulder. She began feeling his arms and chest, exploring the heavy muscles there, squeezing to feel his power. The other glided onto the arm of the sofa to Trevor's left and ran her fingers through his hair.

"The girls are fond of you, sir," Mahmoud told him. "It is not every day they are blessed with a man of your considerable stature."

"Do they speak English?" Trevor asked him. He would much rather Mahmoud wasn't there so that he could enjoy the girls as much as they were enjoying him.

"No, I'm afraid not," Mahmoud drew himself closer to Trevor, leaning across the coffee table. "The Thai people are mostly stupid. Do you know that the Thais are a mongoloid people? Descended from the same stock as Genghis Khan, no less? And I'm sure you know what the term 'mongoloid' means to us in the West. They are like cattle and, just like cattle, they have their uses. Certainly I have grown rich from their sweet milk." He sat back, a beaming smile on his face.

You've grown FAT from their milk, you mean. Trevor was slightly offended that this dirty Arab considered himself to be a westerner. To him he was just a different type of oriental, no better (worse, perhaps) than the Thais.

"Spare me the history lesson, *Prince* Mahmoud. Anyway, it's not their milk I'm interested in," Trevor told him. He made no attempt to hide the disdain from his voice. The small girl on the right had stopped exploring his muscles and decided to caress his crotch instead. A warm surge crept through his groin and he was beginning to stiffen. *Get lost Mahmoud, I'm busy.*

"Yes, let us get down to business," Mahmoud said. "You will have noticed that we have only the finest girls here. Not one of them is older than twenty and the youngest is fourteen, if that is what you fancy. We even have some wonderful girls with perfect breasts and bums . . . and dangly parts between their legs, if you understand my meaning."

"No," Trevor sat up, a little shocked, startling the fondling girls and making them giggle. "I don't want any children or ladyboys. That's not for me."

"Very good, sir, but regardless of what you choose, I must warn you that the girls here are not cheap. If you only wish to spend a few baht then you can find one of the slimy street walkers outside. We ask for a bit more here." Trevor didn't like the sound of that at all. He would much rather take one of the sweet-smelling beauties from Mahmoud's Palace than some dirty skank from outside.

"Money is no object. I'll have the best you can offer." He was eager to get on with it. Maureen had left him with enough money to really enjoy himself. There was no way he could fault her for that. She may have been fifteen years older than him and not much to look at, but she certainly made up for that in pure wealth. That's what had drawn them together in the first place. She wanted a fit, devoted young toy boy and he wanted cash. It was a perfect arrangement, especially when she wasn't around to ruin things. Maureen thought that she had some sort of exclusive rights to him, she had no idea that he strayed whenever he had the chance.

"This way, sir," Mahmoud stood and gestured towards a door beside the stage. Trevor dislodged himself from the girls' fondling and followed Mahmoud towards it. He had to adjust the front of his trousers to make himself more comfortable. The band members had stopped playing and were talking amongst themselves in hushed voices. The raucous laughter of the men with the dancing girls easily drowned out whatever they were saying, but they were looking at Trevor as they spoke. He thought he noticed one of them licking his lips. *He's probably just thirsty . . . unless he's a homo. If he tries it on with me I'll rip his liver out*, he thought as he stepped up to the door held open by Mahmoud.

"We have female clients too," Mahmoud informed him. "They would pay handsomely for a specimen such as you."

Trevor laughed. "I'm sure they would, but I'm not into that. I have enough money." His erection was starting to fade and he was beginning to get bored with *Prince* Mahmoud's conversation.

"As you say, in you go, sir."

"Aren't the girls coming?" He noticed that they'd stayed on the sofa.

"No, sir," Mahmoud looked offended. "I have someone special waiting for you. She is only for the finest patrons."

Trevor liked the sound of that, but she would have to be something really special if she was to surpass the two girls he'd already encountered.

Mahmoud closed the door behind him, and Trevor was far from disappointed. Not only was he glad to finally be rid of Mahmoud's wobbling jowls and his dull conversation, but the sight before him was truly splendid. The room was decorated mostly in lilac and shades of emerald, not entirely to Trevor's taste, but that wasn't what caught his eye.

A slender woman lay languidly across the top of a bed, completely naked. She was like a vision from a dream to Trevor. One of her long legs was pulled up to her midriff, accentuating her smooth curves and hiding her pubic region from sight. Sultry eyes peered through long lashes, inviting Trevor to step closer. She squirmed slightly and patted the bed beside her. Clearly she wanted him to join her. From her eyes Trevor could see that she was as eager as he was, so he didn't waste any time. *I'll have to thank that weird bloke with the sign when this is done*, he thought as he sat himself beside the woman. *Fifty baht may well have been worth it after all.*

"You're fabulous," he said to her and reached out to touch her wonderful thigh. She let out a moan of pleasure, almost inaudible, as his hand slid around to grasp her rounded, tight buttock. He met her eyes and felt himself grow to full arousal. As he leaned in to kiss her neck, she began unbuttoning his shirt. Her fingers felt his tense muscles and her moans grew louder. *She's loving it!* Trevor couldn't believe his luck.

It wasn't long before he was as naked as her, his manhood thrusting forward proudly as he licked and sucked every inch of her. He wanted to taste her, feel her, *enter* her. But before he could position himself between her legs, she rolled over slightly and bent herself forward. She took him into her mouth. Slowly and wetly she teased him, gently sucking and licking at his tip.

Trevor felt himself nearing climax, but there was no way he wanted it to end so soon. He pulled back and removed himself from her. "Not yet," he said. Her tempting eyes were looking up at him, a little disappointed, perhaps.

"Come in me, big boy," she said. Trevor was surprised that she spoke English, but he didn't think about that for too long.

He shook his head, stepped away from the bed and looked around the room. A peculiar looking table was set up beside the bed. It was as narrow as a bench and had handcuffs attached to the bottom of each of its four legs. The top of it was cushioned, like a seat. "What's that for?" he asked almost sheepishly.

"Tied up fun," she told him, climbing to the edge of the bed to be closer to him. She reached out with a hand and took hold of his member, squeezing it gently. "You want to try?"

"A tied-up Thai, eh? Why not?" This was going to be fun.

She smiled and got up from the bed. Trevor delighted in watching as she bent herself over the strange contraption and used his hands to spread her buttocks wide. She giggled and then gasped as he thrust into her pink wetness. He was going at her slowly, savouring the moment. She bobbed along with him, matching his rhythm perfectly. "Why don't you try? You will like," she managed to say between moaning breaths.

Trevor smiled and withdrew himself from her gripping snatch. "Okay, I'll play along."

After she got off the table, Trevor mounted it in the same position that she had been in. His hands were dangling beside the table's front legs, his ankles parallel to the ones at the back. His erection curled around under the table. It was surprisingly comfortable, the cushion on the top felt nice against his bare chest and belly.

The girl wasted no time and quickly closed the handcuffs around Trevor's wrists and ankles. Every time she did so she let out another moan of pleasure, as though she was at the height of ecstasy. Once she was done she positioned herself under the table and took Trevor into her mouth again. She was working at him furiously and it only took a few moments before he was spurting like never before. The added thrill of being strapped to the table only intensified his orgasm.

"That was unbelievable," he breathed heavily after she'd climbed out from underneath him.

She licked her lips. A strange look replaced the sultry one she had previously had on her face. The smile she wore now was terrible and sinister. "He's ready for you now, Mahmoud," she shouted.

"What the hell do you mean?" Trevor tried to get off the table but he couldn't move. The handcuffs were digging painfully into his wrists and ankles as he struggled. "Get me off this fucking thing, you bitch!"

Trevor heard the door open behind him, followed by the sound of many footsteps. The music and laughter were completely gone from the other room.

"Did you enjoy yourself, sir?" It was Mahmoud. Trevor couldn't see him but he recognised the voice.

"What's going on? Get me off this thing."

The whore in front of Trevor started laughing. Some of his semen was still splattered across her cheeks. Mahmoud came to stand beside her, he was laughing too. "Yes, you'll make me a fortune, *sir*," he said.

"Undo these handcuffs or I'll rip your flabby throat out!" Trevor was not amused. He would kill this man if he didn't let him loose.

"Shush, my friend," Mahmoud said to him. "The night is still young and I have many paying guests waiting." He swept his hand towards the door. Trevor strained to look behind him.

It hurt his neck but he had to see what Mahmoud was pointing at.

"No! You can't do this to me!" Trevor thrashed with all his might, but it was hopeless. He couldn't move at all. From behind him a whole group of naked men appeared, some of them were rubbing themselves and licking their lips. Everyone from the other room was there: the band, the westerners and the dancing girls. All of them were smiling, some of the girls were giggling.

"It's not every day we get someone as fine as you through our doors, my friend," Mahmoud told him and started to undress. "I will go first. Don't struggle too much because it's going to be a long night for you, I'm afraid, and you should save your strength for tomorrow. I warned you the price was higher than that charged by the street walkers; you should learn to be more careful, Bangkok can be a dangerous place."

Trevor whimpered and wished he'd settled for the rubber doll, or at least travelled back to Singapore with Maureen.

The Round of the Baskervilles
by Jon Charles

Kirsty told herself to think of the money as she trudged down the final lane to the Woolpack. The last thing she felt like doing that night was yet another evening of being the cheerful barmaid while the regulars at the village's least lively public house sat at the bar. Most would make their sole purchase last a whole evening and try to engage her in conversation while trying to look down her top. But, she needed to make as much money as she could before the new term at university began.

This was going to be the seventh night in a row that she had worked a full shift and given that the night before the pub had been as dead as anything. She had been surprised when Harry had phoned up that afternoon and asked her to go in again. She'd always quite liked Harry as a boss and hoped he wasn't asking her to work because of any lecherous purposes of his own. It was bad enough that she was spending all her evenings with men at least forty years older than her; she didn't need the embarrassment of having to fend off her employer. Needless to say as soon as she finished the call from Harry she got another from an old school friend that she'd happened across in town asking her if she was free that night. She would have had to turn him down anyway - for other reasons - but it still galled her that her social life had reached such a low ebb.

The door creaked with an almost comedic high pitch as Kirsty walked through into the room behind the bar area. It sounded quiet. Well, no surprise there. Moving past the stockpiled boxes of salted peanuts and pork scratchings she opened the next door and stepped into the narrow serving area behind the bar. Harry was cleaning glasses a few steps to her right; more to remove the dust that had gathered she presumed than from their use by the three customers she could see spread along the seats at the bar. She recognised them all from previous evenings and she knew that they had all told her their names as well as asking for hers but she remembered them respectively as Hairy Nostrils Guy, Shouty Voice Man and

Conspiracy Theory Bloke. As well as them there was a young couple she did not recognise at a table in the more dimly-lit corner of the pub. Hardly packed out.

"Kirsty, thanks for coming in," said Harry. "I'm expecting to be busy later on."

"I can see, Harry. Looking rushed off your feet."

"Less of the cheek, girl. Are you okay looking after things for a couple of minutes? I want to walk the dogs and get them settled down for the night."

Kirsty nodded agreement while noting that seven o'clock seemed unusually early for putting the dogs away. Normally Harry let his two large, friendly mongrels have the run of the pub until closing time. After Harry went she looked down the bar to see if any of the regulars needed topping up. Sure enough, Shouty Voice gave her an "Alright Kirsty, love. How about another Guinness?"

Kirsty noticed, as she had on a few previous occasions that the Guinness tap was right in front of where Shouty Voice sat and it was almost impossible to pour without leaning forward. That it was also the pint that took the longest to pull was also, she assumed, no accident.

"I expect you'll soon be back off to university then," said Shouty Voice, seemingly for the benefit not just of Kirsty but also the romantic couple in the corner and anyone who happened to be in the car park.

"Couple of weeks."

"Expect you're looking forward to that. Biology wasn't it?"

"Psychology."

While Shouty Voice launched into a monologue about psychology in sports, Kirsty moved along to clear an empty glass from in front of Hairy Nostrils. She asked him if he wanted another. "Just a half," he replied, his eyes sleepily following her as she served the drink and took the money. To be fair, Hairy Nostrils didn't try to look down her top so much as just look straight at her chest. She had once made the mistake of wearing a nearly transparent blouse and she couldn't remember him making eye contact since.

When Shouty Voice paused to sip from his pint, Conspiracy Theory took the opportunity to explain to him how all sports were fixed and the government knew all about it but chose to do nothing. "Bread and circuses, mate. Bread and circuses."

Kirsty lifted the flap that gave access to the main area of the pub in order to collect glasses from the other two customers, all the while cursing Harry under her breath for summoning her here for this. She was halfway there when she heard the noise of new arrivals outside. The doors opened and five men walked in, one after the other. Leading the group was a silver-grey haired man in, she guessed, his fifties. He had a neatly-trimmed beard with a touch of red among the grey. Behind him came a clean-shaven man of similar age and then three younger men all looking somewhere in their twenties. All turned to smile at her as they padded across the floor and seated themselves down at a large table in the open space in the centre of the pub. They talked quietly among themselves for a couple of minutes before the bearded man strolled over to the bar. Putting down the glasses she had collected from the romantic couple, Kirsty stood ready to take their order. Alone amongst the customers, so far that evening, he looked her in the eyes.

The bearded man smiled as he looked at Kirsty and then, studying the chalk board list of local scrumpy ciders, he made a request for five pints of 'Widow's Despair'.

"We normally only serve that in half-pints."

The bearded man said nothing but smiled at her again. Shrugging her shoulders, Kirsty started pulling five pints of the strong cider. When she went to ring up the order on the till Shouty Voice whispered to her. "Do you know who they are?" Kirsty shook her head hoping that the new arrivals would not hear themselves being talked about but Shouty Voice continued in hushed mode. "The Baskervilles."

Kirsty shrugged to try and show it meant little to her. She handed the change to the bearded man and watched as he carried a tray of pint glasses back to the rest of his group. "Get your paws around these," she heard him say.

The group of five was already on their second round of strong cider when Harry returned from walking his dogs. Kirsty demonstrated her best barmaid laugh while hissing under her breath. "Who the hell are these Baskervilles, Harry?"

"Good customers, Kirsty, love. They come here every now and again and spend lots of money, get drunk and never cause trouble. Just keep serving the rounds and smile and I dare say they'll give you a decent tip at the end of the night."

Shouty Voice waited until Harry had gone and then gestured for Kirsty to come nearer. "I don't care what Harry says, the Baskervilles have an odd reputation. These days they just come back for the occasional visit, all together like, but they used to live around here. All sorts of stuff about them being abnormal somehow, the old folks in the village say; those that remember them."

It was only half past seven when the request for a third round was made. This time it was one of the younger men who came to the bar. His voice was soft and low and his eyes a piercing blue leaving Kirsty requiring less effort than usual to appear gregarious.

"Can I ask," Kirsty said, "whether you're all celebrating something?"

The man with the blue eyes appeared unsure what to say. Kirsty instantly regretted having asked the question but then he started to speak.

"No. Not really. More of a ritual really. If anything we're trying to forget something."

"Oh, I'm sorry. It's just that you all seemed in quite good spirits. There's been lots of laughter coming from your table."

"Trying to forget something need not be an unhappy thing," said the man. "I realise this may be hard to believe, what with the strong cider and all, but we are doing this so that we don't hurt anybody." He took the glasses and walked back to the others.

The noise level went up and the other customers started to drift away. Shouty Voice went first after telling Kirsty to make sure Harry forked out for a taxi to get her home that night. Next was Conspiracy Theory who left with a parting gift of a knowing wink. Kirsty did not know what knowledge the knowing wink was supposed to reference and the temptation to enquire was not strong. Finally, Hairy Nostrils mumbled "G'night," and shuffled off into the night.

Kirtsy collected more empty glasses from the Baskervilles and the couple in the corner. The latter were just getting up and putting on their coats. The man said thank you and the girl told her they were off for a walk in the moonlight.

"Enjoy. It's bright tonight."

After serving an eighth round of drinks to the five men, Kirsty asked Harry what time he expected her to stay until.

"I was hoping you could stay until closing time so you can take your half of the tip."

More requests for drinks followed. The younger men took it in turns to stagger over to the bar, with increasingly lolloping gaits. The men were clearly reaching an advanced stage of inebriation but, curiously, none of them was getting rowdy or out of control. If anything their voices got quieter. They even seemed to make less noise as they walked.

What turned out to be the final round was bought by the younger man Kirsty had spoken to earlier. Despite the large amount of alcohol he had consumed, his eyes retained their clear quality and he managed to maintain eye contact while smiling disarmingly. He told her she smelled nice. Kirsty tried to laugh it off but the telltale signs had been building as the evening had progressed. She watched him walk back to the others sensing that he knew what she was doing.

As the Baskervilles helped each other to their feet, Kirsty collected the glasses and noted a couple of large denomination notes sitting in the centre of their table. Four of the men divided into pairs, putting their arms around each other in order to be able to make use of four legs rather than two as they made their way to the door. The bearded man who had led them into the pub at the start of the evening remained still for a few moments. "Please accept the money to make up for any inconvenience we have caused." And then, he too left.

Harry took the glasses from her at the bar. "I'll sort these out. You get yourself home."

Kirsty didn't argue. The night sky was clear as she walked through the pub car park. Someone had spray painted a letter F between the L and the P on the pub sign. There was a people carrier parked close to a hedge that had not been there when she arrived earlier. She could see no sign of anyone in or near it. Kirsty looked up at the stars and full moon. She looked around for the footprints that she knew would be there and followed them across the gravel. She could hear the now familiar voices in the distance ahead of her and she followed, through a gap in the hedge and across the adjacent field. Her nostrils flared. She was getting closer to them, she knew, even though she could no longer hear the voices. When she was close enough she started to unbutton her blouse.

Bare feet padding silently across the grass, Kirsty reached the Baskervilles. Like her, they were all now naked. Unlike her they were all asleep. Some, possibly all, were snoring. The change was starting but the convulsions, the rapid growth of hair and shocking transformations to their bodies, did not wake any of them. *Typical* thought Kirsty as she started to prowl around the unconscious lupine figures, *I finally meet some men I have something in common with and they all pass out on me.* She sat down, rested her head on her front paws and offered up a soft howl to the moon.

Rosemary's Baby Shower
by Ken MacGregor

Another perfect woman breezed past Rosemary. "You're *glowing!*" Janet said over her shoulder as she crossed the room to add her silver-wrapped box to the mountain of gifts.

Rosemary smiled at Janet's back and rested one hand on her bulging midsection. *In the event of the Zombie Apocalypse,* Rosemary thought, *we can use the gift boxes as a barricade.* She never used to think about zombies. That was Neal's fault; he had a basement full of canned food, bottled water and weapons. *I know zombies aren't real,* he'd say, *but what if they are?* Carrying his child was affecting her mind. Rosemary smiled. She wished Neal were here now, even though she knew he hated this kind of thing.

Janet set her gift high on the pile and swept back to Rosemary. Janet was a one-woman floor show; every action was dripping with drama. Janet half squatted, half bent by Rosemary's chair, knees together; she managed to make the awkward pose look elegant. Janet leaned in and gave her very pregnant friend a hug. Rosemary hugged her back and both women did air kisses at each other's cheeks. She kept it to herself, but Rosemary still found the air-kissing pretty ridiculous.

"You're so beautiful, honey," Janet said.

"I'm so fat," Rosemary shot back, laughing. "But, thank you. It's good to see you. How's Rob?"

Janet made a face.

"I'm sure I wouldn't know," she said. Her voice was arctic.

They split up, Rosemary thought, *again.* Rosemary didn't want to get roped into another lengthy discussion of Rob's many faults so she let it drop. Besides, everyone was here now. It was time to get the party started.

"Thanks, you guys," Rosemary said, "for coming. Someone brought a forklift and semi to haul the gifts, right?" Her friends laughed. "And maybe another one for this!" Rosemary grabbed two handfuls of her belly. More laughter.

"Rosemary," Gina raised her hand like a fourth-grader. "Is it a boy or a girl? Do you know?" The other women speculated in quick whispers.

Rosemary smiled. "I do know," she said, pausing to draw out the suspense. "It's a girl!" Some of them actually shrieked. Rosemary was covered in congratulations and hugs and quick kisses and her nose was assaulted with nine different kinds of perfume. Rosemary had grown to love most of these women, but sometimes she still felt like an alien among them. Getting used to Neal's family had been hard enough, but her new friends were a real challenge.

Rosemary had grown up near the bottom end of middle class. Her parents still rented an apartment; they probably could have managed a modest house by the time they retired, but didn't seem to want the hassle. Neal grew up in a house the size of her parents' whole building.

They probably would have never crossed paths if not for Neal's love of theatre and Rosemary's passion for acting. Neal saw her on stage and he fell for her hard. Rosemary took some convincing, but Neal was so sweet and kind and thoughtful; he was also persistent and rich, neither of which hurt. Finally, he wore Rosemary down and she agreed to go out with him, just to shut him up, she told herself. Turns out, Neal was a lot of fun: he made Rosemary laugh and he made her feel beautiful, and that first date led to more. When Neal proposed nine months after they met, Rosemary was happy to accept. Now, she was about to have his baby, and she was surrounded by his friends.

Rosemary's two closest friends from before her current life were both out of town they said, sending their regrets. Rosemary wondered if they were making excuses because they felt uncomfortable with this crowd. *Hell*, Rosemary thought, *I wouldn't blame them. I know just how they feel.* Still, she missed Tabby and Helena and wished they were here.

Gina brought Rosemary a small plate of goodies from the snack table; there were some raw carrots and cucumbers and a piece of chocolate. The candy was both bitter and sweet with a hint of orange; it was like nothing Rosemary had tasted and she was on the fence about whether she liked it. Frankly, she'd rather have a Snickers.

For the next half hour or so, they played baby shower games, most of which Rosemary found cute if asinine. The only one she enjoyed was the *Tinkle in the Pot* game, where a woman had to hold a quarter between her knees and cross five feet of floor to drop it in a mason jar. To be a good sport, Rosemary did it too; she made it to the jar, but completely missed the drop. The fact that Rosemary couldn't even see her knees might have been part of the problem. That was pretty hilarious; Rosemary fell into giggling fits. She laughed so hard, for so long she wondered if she would ever stop. Gasping for breath, Rosemary regained control; her cheeks were sore and she had a mild stitch in her side. Only one woman made it in, Beverly, and she nearly split her dress throwing her arms up in a V for Victory.

Rosemary excused herself to go pee. Her bladder felt only slightly bigger than a quarter these days, and the laughing had made it worse. When she stood up, Rosemary felt light-headed. She held the back of her chair for a moment until it cleared. Gina gave Rosemary a look that seemed like calculated concern. Rosemary wondered what the other woman was thinking, but had more pressing matters to attend to. She had a pleasant buzzing in her brain that made the discomfort of her bladder fade. Still, Rosemary knew she'd better go soon or she'd have an embarrassing accident. After, she washed her hands and looked at her reflection for a moment. She really did kind of glow. Though that may have been the fluorescent lights. She had a big goofy smile on her lips and wasn't sure why. Rosemary dried her hands and returned to the party. She stopped cold after opening the door.

Her new friends - all thirteen of them - were naked. Their dresses and undergarments were neatly folded over chairs. Rosemary's jaw dropped a little; she had no idea what to say or do. For a moment, she stared at the women. Rosemary took in their well-toned bodies, their Brazilian waxes, their perfect breasts. These were the best physiques money could buy. Finally, Rosemary found her voice.

"Um," she said. "I don't think I've heard of this game." She smiled to show she could be a good sport. Gina stepped forward and touched Rosemary's belly. Rosemary flinched. She was thinking, *I'm in a room full of crazy people.* But the normal, physical reactions, the increased pulse, adrenaline were oddly absent. Rosemary felt detached from the weirdness in front of her, like she couldn't bring herself to be more than mildly surprised.

"Oh, honey," Gina said. "There are so many things you have yet to learn." Gina stroked Rosemary's midsection with both hands. She leaned forward, her breasts resting on Rosemary's own, her breath on Rosemary's cheek. Rosemary was a bit stunned; she was in alien territory. Rosemary felt outside herself, and she couldn't seem to make herself react to this properly.

"I'm not," Rosemary began. "I mean, I don't, um, like girls really. I'm okay with it; it's just not for me, you know? No offense."

Gina leaned back, eyes sparkling. "We're not lesbians, silly," Gina said. "We're priestesses."

Rosemary shook the cobwebs out of her head. She took a step back away from Gina and the other naked women. She put a hand on her belly protectively.

"Let me guess: priestesses of Satan?" Rosemary asked. She thought she might already know the answer.

"Don't be ridiculous," Gina answered. "Satan is a ridiculous myth fostered by early Christians to cast a poor light on the image of the Pagan god The Horned One. We are priestesses of Lilith."

"Oh," Rosemary said. "I forget who that is."

"The real first woman," Gina said. "Created as Adam's equal. You know, before the chick from his rib showed up. Lilith left both Adam and Eden. She represents independence, feminism, righteousness; Lilith is the fire in every woman's loins."

"Right," Rosemary said. "Sure. I knew that." She smirked, but sobered when she saw the other women's expressions.

"You're sceptical," Gina said. "Of course you are. I understand. But, my dear, sweet Rosemary, you have no idea. Neal has been groomed his whole life for this. He was chosen for his strong genes and was raised to understand his role. In turn, Neal chose you for your beauty and your passion. You will be mother to the new Lilith, my dear. And, when she grows up, the men of this world will tremble."

"Neal?" Rosemary asked, trying to wrap her head around this whole thing. "He never said anything. Wait. Why are you naked?"

"Oh," Gina said. "Yeah. That must seem odd. We just don't want to get blood on our dresses." Gina stepped to the table of food and picked up the carving knife; she wiped it carefully with a linen napkin from the hilt to the end of the blade. Rosemary stepped back, but two other naked women blocked the only door.

"Please," Rosemary said. "I'll join your coven or whatever. I'll worship Lilith. But, please, don't kill me or hurt my baby."

This was met with silence. Then, Gina's eyes widened. She laughed, and kept laughing, so hard she had to put her hands on her knees to stay upright. Rosemary wondered if Gina would accidentally cut her own leg with the knife. Then Rosemary thought that if she did cut herself, Rosemary could use the resulting confusion to escape. Finally, she got exasperated.

"Gina," Rosemary said. "What's so damn funny?" Gina got control of herself; she had the hiccups. It made Rosemary smile to see this naked woman holding a carving knife and hiccupping every few seconds. Rosemary idly wondered if maybe she was losing her mind.

"It's for the umbilical cord, silly," Gina said. "We cut the cord, tie it off and pass the baby around. Each of us will give her our blessing and we hand her back to her mother. You. Babies come out messy, and the most efficient way to clean off is to simply shower. I can't believe you thought the knife was for you." Every fourth or fifth word was interrupted by a *hic*.

"Well," Rosemary said, hands on her hips. "You have to admit this whole thing is kind of weird. How did you expect me to react?" She felt her face get hot. It was the first normal reaction she'd had to anything in a long time.

"I'm sorry, honey," Janet said from over by the gift boxes. "We keep forgetting you don't come from money." A few of the other women nodded, as if this explained everything.

"All rich people do this sort of thing?" Rosemary was incredulous.

"Yeah," Gina said. "Pretty much. We bore easily. Okay, Rosemary. Please take off your *hic* dress so we can get started. I would hate to see it ruined."

Beverly, a woman Rosemary had only ever spoken to maybe once, unzipped Rosemary from behind. The other women moved up to help and pretty soon Rosemary was naked, too. She hadn't been in the sun for months, and her skin was very pale. Rosemary's swollen breasts rested atop her distended belly; the muscles of her arms and legs were encased in fat and tight skin. She felt like an albino harp seal among eels.

"Here," Gina said. "Eat this." She held a chocolate truffle up to Rosemary's nose. It smelled wonderful. Rosemary inched forward about to bite and stopped. She gave Gina the stink-eye.

"What is it?" Rosemary asked.

"It will induce labour," Gina said.

Rosemary nodded. It was what she expected, but she wasn't prepared for the honest answer. She was due in a week anyway, so it should be okay. *What the hell?* she thought and took the candy from Gina with her teeth. It was delicious. In the back of her mind, Rosemary understood that she was reacting too calmly to all of this. She wondered if she was in shock.

"How long do we ..." Rosemary began, then she felt a loosening inside herself, a shifting. "Oh my god. That was fast." The women around Rosemary helped her to a squatting position. Someone brought a big plastic tarp from somewhere and slid it under Rosemary. She lifted one foot and then the other so the tarp could be spread. Rosemary felt calm, despite the lunacy of the situation, and she wondered if maybe there was something else in that chocolate.

"Did you drug me?" Rosemary asked Gina. The other woman nodded. Again with the honest answer.

"Long time ago," Gina said. "With that first chocolate."

Rosemary wanted to be shocked, appalled, but couldn't muster the indignation. Whatever they gave her let her think clearly, but made it so she didn't much mind what was going on. *Man,* Rosemary thought, *the street value of this stuff would be epic. Makes you feel at peace with the world. They could call it World Peace.* She giggled, the sound seeming girlish to her own ears.

Rosemary felt her baby turn over so its head was down, as if it knew just how this whole thing was supposed to go. Rosemary felt her daughter move inside, straining against the too small space to get out. It hurt like hell, but Rosemary was detached from the pain. Like she was watching a graphic movie of someone else giving birth and feeling empathetic twinges in her own body. A mess of fluid, blood and placenta splashed out of Rosemary onto the plastic sheet. The women closest to Rosemary were splattered with gore. None of them seemed to mind, adding to the surreal quality of the whole thing. The pressure was intense, and real pain hit all at once. Then, it was over.

The tiny life, covered in white, pasty vernix was in Janet's hands. Beverly attached a small orange clamp on the umbilical cord; it looked like the kind you might get at Home Depot. Gina severed the cord with a neat flick of the blade. Janet passed the baby to Gina, who held her for a moment, supporting her tiny head and then passed her on. The child was breathing, but silent. Finally, it was Rosemary's turn. She had sat down in her own filth, exhausted but still somehow okay with everything. Rosemary hoped this drug would last until she had a chance to sleep; she didn't want it to wear off and have the pain and her normal reactions come back all at once.

Rosemary held her baby to her own bare skin. She felt that this was the way nature intended childbirth: naked and raw and honest. Rosemary helped the girl's tiny round mouth find the nipple and got her to latch on right away. The mother was filled with pride and love for her daughter. She forgot for the moment the thirteen naked women in the room.

"Welcome to the world, Lilith," Gina said. The others repeated it like a prayer. It was a bit creepy, actually.

"What if I want to call her something else?" Rosemary asked. There was a challenge in her voice.

"Go ahead," Gina said. "It doesn't matter. It won't change who she is."

Rosemary looked at her suckling baby for a long moment. She gently stroked the miniature facial features. *She has my ears*, Rosemary thought. *Thank God she didn't get Neal's*. She smiled and looked up at Gina.

"Lilith is a fine name," Rosemary said. She looked down again at her baby. The teeny girl cracked open her eyes; they were orange and had vertical pupils, like a cat's. They were strange, those eyes, inhuman but beautiful. Rosemary knew that this was all crazy, that she was in the middle of something completely fucked up. She knew all that, but as she held her baby, her stunning little bundle of life, she didn't care.

"Gina," Rosemary said without looking up, "will she really change the world?"

Gina and the other priestesses would groom Lilith to be powerful, influential and charismatic. The tiny baby girl would grow to be a leader of women; if things went according to plan, Lilith would bring about the end of the patriarchy. There would, of course be resistance; there would likely be blood, and a lot of it. However, Gina didn't want to burden the young mother, so she kept these thoughts to herself.

"Count on it," Gina said.

"Well," Rosemary said to her baby, "what mother could ask for more?

Twi-tard
by Scott Harper

"Hah! Vampires are the biggest pussies!" Turac snorted, slamming his meaty paw down with supernatural force onto the bar. Glasses shattered and beer sprayed across the entire counter and onto the floor. Startled by the crash, a giant flesh golem jumped out of his chair and focused his dead grey eyes on Turac. Not intimidated by the undead creature, the werewolf snarled at the golem, black lips raised and fangs bared. The golem hesitated for a second, then threw his stitched hands up in surrender and sat back down.

Creese rolled his eyes up and then looked down at his broken beer mug, a sigh escaping his lips. *Here we go again*, he thought, anticipating Turac's weekly diatribe.

Turac punched Creese in the arm to get his attention, then pointed at the television set above the bar. On the screen, a teenage girl stared longingly at a pale, scrawny middle-aged guy who appeared completely out of place in a high school classroom. Creese looked up and recognized the film; the hugely successful but fatally flawed series that had turned the public spotlight on his kind in the worst sort of way.

"Look at this douchebag! All he does is brood and whine about how he can never be with a human. 'Oh, poor me! I'd kiss you but I'm afraid I'll bite your head off.' What the hell is that? When did vampires decide to start playing with their food? Makes me want to puke! Worthless piece of crap!" Turac slammed his paw on the bar again to make his point. More beer soaked the floor.

Knowing Turac was just getting warmed up, Creese shook his head and looked back at his broken mug, wishing he had stayed home.

"What? Got nothing to say? Just sit there like a punk bitch shaking your head. Jesus! You're as big a pussy as that guy in the movie. These last few years, all you do is sulk and tell me how tired you are. 'No Turac, I can't go out with you. I've got to lay here in my coffin and mope over the curse of my eternal existence.' I can't believe you even came out with me tonight."

Creese already regretted his decision to accompany the werewolf to the bar. He had initially resisted Turac's insistence that they go out, content to sit at home with a mystery novel and some pig's blood. Not willing to take no for an answer, Turac decided to make his point by marking his territory all over Creese's tiny apartment. The vampire quickly relented.

Turac turned his attention back to the TV. "I thought vampires were supposed to be super-intelligent, living forever and all that crap. Look at this dumbass, he's over a hundred years old and he's still in high school." A small smile curled Turac's muzzle. "This guy reminds me of you."

Creese winced at the werewolf's gibe as he turned away to scan the bar, seeing a mix of humans and supernaturals drinking and talking together. Turac's comments had sparked a memory of a time long ago when Creese's bloodsire had turned him – right at the cusp of manhood, condemning him to life as an eternal teenager cursed with the knowledge of ages.

"Hey pussy!" Turac yelled, trying to get Creese's attention. "Remember the good old days when you used your fangs for something more than a bottle opener? Remember when we would go out to hunt under the full moon rather than sulk at a bar, picking off humans like they were fruit and gorging ourselves until we puked? I remember that ass-kicking bloodsucker, not this limp-wristed Twi-tard wannabee."

Yeah, I remember those time too, Creese admitted to himself. The rush of adrenaline hit Creese's veins as images of the past made their way through the fog of melancholy. *I remember when we took on the Knights Templar. They were supposed to be the elite fighting force of their time. I always loved the sound of screeching metal and popping chainmail as we ripped apart their armour. The smell of sweat and blood as they screamed and I sunk my hands into their flesh. The amazing wet tearing sound and then the throb of a heart pulsing in my hand. And the taste of blood, just like liquid nirvana, driving away the eternal cold.*

I remember another time when we hunted the Red Coats. We were flying up a hillside, the trees just a blur as our legs propelled us towards our prey. There wasn't any pain as the lead bullets tore through us, maybe a slight sting like a static shock. I can't forget the rush of running into battle, slapping aside muskets and sabres. I loved ripping away their red coats to reveal the fragile necks underneath, the fluttering just below the skin, knowing what lay beneath. There is nothing like the first bite, sinking fangs into their arteries and the screams and the thrashing and the terror. The roar of victory we shared, raising our dead prizes to the full moon. Yes, I do remember.

For a second, the adrenaline rush fuelled by his memories awoke a sense of invulnerability in Creese that had been squashed by the weight of ennui from centuries of existence. He began to see how ridiculous his current situation had become. The years of stagnation, giving up his will to live, all now seemed like a bad joke.

Turac slammed Creese across his back, jarring his attention back to the present. "Oh, this is too rich," the lycanthrope chortled. Creese looked up to the screen. The middle-aged vampire had removed his shirt and was standing in the sun, the light reflecting off him like a diamond. "Tell me please that you don't sparkle like that in the sun. Just like Tinkerbell!"

Just the spark he needed, Creese released his smothered rage and all the frustration that had built up over the last few decades and let it pour over him. His thin white hand shot out like a snake, wrapping itself around the werewolf's muscle-corded neck. He squeezed, then lifted Turac off the ground, watching as the wolfman's eyes bugged out. With a snap of his wrist, Creese flung the three-hundred-pound werewolf across the bar into a group of tables. The demons seated there scattered as Turac smashed through their dinner of zebra carcass and pig intestines. One demon slipped on the slimy entrails and slammed into a robed warlock. Trying to catch his balance, the warlock reached for a chair and unintentionally unleashed a bolt of flame from his fingers, setting the chair on fire. As the flames spread, they found their way to the spilled alcohol on the floor and quickly the bar ignited into a roaring blaze. Panic set in as humans and supernaturals scattered to escape. The flesh golem, unable to see through the smoke, smashed through the wall and tumbled onto the street, inadvertently creating an escape route for others.

Turac quickly pulled himself up from the broken tables, flinging zebra parts from his matted fur. "Look who just woke up. I was wondering what it would take to get a rise out of you, deadboy. Well, you just bit off more than you can chew. I'm going to suck out your eyeballs!"

The lycanthrope launched himself at Creese, slamming his paws down on the vampire's chest and burying his maw into Creese's throat. Creese felt his flesh yield under the assault of iron claws and razor fangs. As he was pushed back against the flaming wreckage of the bar, his clothing now on fire, the words of his bloodsire came unbidden to him. "*Never forget what you are. Apex predator.*" Creese's eyes flashed red as he grabbed Turac's claws, tearing the deadly daggers out of his chest, then headbutted the werewolf away from his throat.

"*Unaging. Undying. Immortal.*"

The jagged gashes Turac had inflicted on Creese's chest and neck healed instantly, the skin suddenly white and smooth and unlined..

"*Armed always with the strength of twenty men.*"

Creese backhanded the werewolf, sending teeth flying across the room. The huge beast smashed to the ground, a whimper escaping his shattered snout. Creese was on him instantly, his fanged teeth unsheathed as he tore into Turac's neck. Warm, powerful blood flowed into him, eating away the cold that had dulled his senses, filling him with even greater strength. His own beast, the red-thirst, demanded more.

Just as Creese was about to give in to his beast, through the smoke he could see Turac's paw tapping the floor, a universally recognized sign of submission. Above the roar of the flames he heard Turac scream, "I give, I give. Uncle, uncle. Ahhgodd, don't kill me you crazy sunuvabitch!" Creese took a deep breath, taking a minute to bring his beast back under control. As his fangs retracted, he sat back on his heels and looked at his broken friend on the floor. Creese then stood and offered his hand to the defeated werewolf.

"Jesus Christ, I thought you were gonna kill me." Turac took Creese's hand and stood, his tail tucked. A crooked smile played on the lycanthrope's broken face as he reverted to his human form. "Was wondering what it would take for you to come around."

As Creese and Turac turned to leave the burning bar, they noticed the smoke was changing from black to white. In the centre of the bar, a warlock had summoned a water elemental to put out the flame. As the fire receded and the smoke cleared, the bar patrons began to return as though nothing had happened. Creese smiled, happy to have been able to finally let loose. He felt as if the weight of the world had been lifted from his shoulders. Turac massaged his rapidly healing neck and looked up to the TV.

"I knew that shitty movie had to be good for something."

edited by Stephanie Ellis & S.G. Mulholland

Cycle Killer
by Nick Walters

"Are you really going to start this thing with Penelope again?" said my wife. She bit into her toast and fixed me with The Glare.

"Yeah, I think so." I sipped my tea (no sugar - I'll never get used to that).

Crunch. Crunch. "Really?"

"Yes, really! I don't see any harm in it."

Beth put the toast down. "It's too risky. You might get hurt."

"Rubbish!" I snorted. "As long as I take it steady, I'll be fine. And I know Penelope will be gentle with me."

Beth abandoned the toast. "Well I don't advise it."

I looked in envy at the butter glistening in the morning sun. "It'll be good for me. And I need the exercise." I patted my burgeoning tum.

Beth stood up and regarded me with a mixture of pity and - well, just pity, really. "There are better and less dangerous ways of losing weight."

"But not as much fun!"

Beth picked up her briefcase. "Look, I haven't got time to argue now, can we discuss this later? And don't do anything rash."

"I'm going to see Penelope," I called after her. "Might even take her out!"

Beth didn't reply. I waited until I'd heard the front door slam and, a few moments later, her car start up and pull away. I finished my tea and then hauled myself upstairs. The cruel glass slab of the bathroom scales awaited. I touched them with the toe of my slipper to activate them, and then sloughed off my dressing-gown until I stood naked before the altar of doom. I stepped on--the glass cold against my bare soles--and glanced down as the digits resolved themselves. Fifteen stone and seven, no, eight. Two up from yesterday. Big sigh. I dressed in my forty-inch waist jeans and tried to ignore my flabby neck and jowls in the mirror as I shaved. The heart attack was over three months ago now and I'd been steadily building up my exercise routine, walking every day as soon as I was advised to, but I felt I needed to do more. Needed Penelope.

I wasn't going to go mad. Not at first. Take it slowly. Not do anything today, maybe. Just look at her, touch her, feel her, get re-acquainted with her after all this time. We'd been steady partners right up until the heart attack, and I missed her terribly.

Once dressed I went outside to the garage. I hadn't driven since the attack as Beth insisted on taking the wheel. Fair enough, as I was prone to a spot of road rage. I squeezed past my car, cold and hard and reassuring against my thighs, to the back of the garage where all the junk was stored.

There she was, abandoned behind an old ironing board and half-buried underneath clammy plastic bags of back issues of The Economist. It had only been a few months and already she was buried alive.

I heaved the bags away and the contents went slithering to the oily floor. I grimaced at the odour of damp mould. I thrust the ironing board clattering aside, panting with the effort and excitement, and grabbed hold of Penelope. She was cold beneath my fingers. I should have moved the car to enable me to get her out of the garage but I was far too impatient. I lifted her up and swung her over the boot into the gap between the car and the dusty breeze-block garage wall. She was now in front of me and I somehow managed to manhandle and cajole her into the bright sunlight.

I leaned her against the bonnet and stood back to look at her. Apart from a few cobwebs, she wasn't too bad. Her pale blue paintwork still looked as good as new, apart from a few chinks and nips, but that was only to be expected. Her tyres were flat, and her chain needed oiling, but those things were also to be expected after so many weeks of neglect.

I retrieved a duster from the house and set to work clearing away the crap. Penelope was an old steel-frame Raleigh, the sort they didn't make any more, heavier than these modern models but far more comfortable. She'd been my companion for almost three decades, my friend in those dark, single days before Beth. More reliable than a human friend. Trustworthy, stalwart, the perfect partner. We had ridden thousands of miles together. My eyes teared up as I worked, thinking back to all those good rides, fearing that my riding days were over.

Sod that. Heart attack or no heart attack, I was only forty-five, still young, still relatively fit. All I needed to do was lose a bit of weight and soon Penelope and I would be flying together once more up and hill and down dale.

I couldn't find the GT-85 so I had to use 3-in-1 oil and I whispered apologies as I applied it to Penelope's chain. I then found the foot-pump and got her tyres nice and hard, 80 PSI.

And then she was ready.

Could I?

I looked up. The sky was clear, the early September breeze kissing my upturned face. Summer was coming to an end and the nights were drawing in. Best to make the most of the good weather while it lasted. I wouldn't go far, just to the end of the close and back, not even a quarter of a mile. I just couldn't bear to put Penelope straight back into the garage.

I usually wear shorts and cycling shoes (I don't do clipless and never will, can't stand the feeling of not being able to put my foot down) but now I was just in trainers, jeans and an old sweatshirt. It would do. I closed the garage door, and, looking around to see if any of the neighbours were watching (nosy sods) I wheeled Penelope into the road. Up onto the saddle (sprung leather, much more comfortable than plastic), feet on the pedals, then I sat for a while, getting used to the feel of her again. Despite its comforting attributes the leather saddle hurt my bum bone and it felt strange to be back here after so long convalescing. My weight bore down on my hands on the handlebars and I felt like a giant sack of spuds.

I raised my head and gazed down the close. The neat red brick houses and postage stamp lawns, the shining cars in the drives. I could hear the distant rumble and blare of the traffic on the High Street and I yearned be out there with it, under that sky, with Penelope's wheels eating up the miles.

With a grunt I pushed off and wobbled out from the kerb. Selecting the granny gear I began to pedal, and for a glorious moment it all came back, my muscle memory adapting instantly to Penelope, and Penelope herself seeming to thrum with life. I was soon at the end of the close. This was easy! I'd go into town and back. Maybe even further! What was to stop me? Cycling isn't hard on the heart; unlike running there are periods of rest built in when you're coasting. It's the perfect aerobic exercise, and kind on your knees, also unlike running. What better exercise could I want?

Encouraged by these lofty thoughts I turned right into Rood Lane. This was a narrow street lined with former miners' cottages, and led up a slight incline. I pushed harder on the pedals, slightly mortified that I needed to put extra effort in. Gritting my teeth I put my back into it and my right foot seemed to go straight through the pedal. I was pitched forward, my chest hit the handlebars and then I was on the ground, Penelope on top of me.

I lay there for a while, staring up at the sky, horribly aware of the pain in the centre of my chest. Was I having another attack? My breathing was okay, and the pain began to spread out a bit. I realised it was probably where my chest had hit the bars. There'd be a bruise in the morning. I eased Penelope off me and sat up. I winced as a sharp pain manifested in my right shin. My jeans were dark with blood and I rolled them up to see an inch long gash, thankfully not too deep. From the jagged pattern it looked like Penelope's chainring had cut into me as I'd fallen. I picked her up and staggered to the side of the road. I felt the outer chainring, the big one. It was greasy with oil but the teeth felt knife-sharp. My gaze moved to the inner chainring, the smaller one, which I'd been on when the accident happened. Something was wrong and it took my dazed brain seconds to realise that there was no chain!

I stepped back and saw that the chain was trailing along the tarmac like an oily mechanical snake. It had obviously snapped and threw me over the bars. It was three, four years old, should have replaced it a year or so ago. Probably best it broke now rather than when I was going at speed downhill, or with traffic. I winced as I thought of the horrendous accident that could have happened. Then I picked up the chain and slung it in a nearby skip.

With as much dignity as I could muster I limped home and cleaned myself up. I took Penelope into the house vaguely promising myself I'd put her back in the garage later.

I made myself a cup of tea and then, after all this excitement, fell asleep on the sofa.

I woke a few hours later, feeling light-headed and a bit sick, so I made myself lunch (tuna and cucumber sandwiches on wholemeal bread, healthy and filling) and then took Penelope's front wheel off and put it and her in the boot of my car, ready to take to Ed's Cycles in the morning. I put a plaster over the cut on my leg, which had crusted over nicely. Beth was bound to notice, but I'd invent some lie about a patch of eczema that I'd scratched and made bleed. She need never know about my abortive first ride.

How I underestimate that woman!

She came home from work in a savage rage, slamming the front door and hurling her briefcase onto the sofa where I sat watching Homes Under The Hammer. The briefcase bounced off the sofa and clumped to the floor.

"You stupid fucking idiot!" she bellowed.

I thought immediately that this is not the way to behave towards a heart attack victim, then it occurred to me that she might actually be trying to induce another one. I decided to play innocent. 'What?'

She paced up and down the living room, clenching and unclenching her fists. "Fucking Penelope! Sally saw you. Saw it all!"

Damn those nosy neighbours. "Well, why didn't she come out to help me, then?"

Beth ignored this. "How could you be so irresponsible?"

I began to lose my own temper. "Look, it was only to the end of the close and back! How was I to know the chain was going to go? You can't predict these things!"

"And that's exactly why you should give up cycling! You never know when some idiot is going to cut you up or step out in front of you or open a car door in your path!"

I stood up. "Rubbish. That's life, you could say that about anything. If you thought like that you'd never leave the bloody house! Existence is risk."

She stopped pacing and stood glaring at me. "Are you all right?"

"Yes, fine, a small cut on my leg. It's Penelope who really suffered."

She stepped forward and hugged me. She mumbled into my neck. "Sorry. Bad case today."

I hugged her back. "It's okay, it's okay."

I then made us both a cup of tea and waited until she had calmed down.

I brought the subject up again as the pasta for evening dinner was simmering away. Beth stood in the kitchen staring out of the window, clearly deep in thought, so I went to stand beside her.

"I'm going to go on with it, you know. With Penelope."

She turned to me, frowning, but I held up a hand. "Look, it's good exercise and something I love doing. I wish you'd get a bike too." Cycling was something Beth never took to; swimming was her thing. And kickboxing. "Tell you what, I'll leave it until my next check-up and make sure it's OK."

Beth was fine with that.

Inwardly, I exulted.

Penelope and I would soon be back together again.

***

I was true to my word, I left it until I'd seen the cardio before I next took Penelope out. They were okay with it, with the usual warnings to take it very easy and stop if I noticed any adverse effects. My heart attack was relatively mild and I had not lost a lot of heart muscle. I was still on beta blockers to manage the heart rate and was doing OK. The main thing you get after a heart attack is tiredness – for two months I was sleepy almost all of the time and it was only in the last month or so that I began to feel anything approaching normal. I think I was beginning get lazy, to adjust to feeling bad, and of course I was putting on more weight and I needed to lose that – being overweight had led to the heart attack in the first place, and the cardio was worried that I wasn't shedding it quickly enough.

So all things considered I was going to take it very, very easy.

The first ride I did was two weeks after the accident, when I got Penelope back from Ed's Cycles. I dressed in my proper cycling gear: hard-soled cycling/walking shoes, black lycra shorts, blue and black cycling jersey (that felt a bit tight), and black leather fingerless cycling gloves.

The sense of elation when I pushed away from the kerb on a newly-serviced machine! Bliss. I sailed out of the close, up Rood Street and through the town, staying in low gears and enjoying the feeling of being back in the saddle. Clowne was a small but busy little town, densely populated, which meant traffic could be a nightmare. I'd forgotten how abusive some drivers could be, and even on this short trip I had someone bawl "off the road, cunt!" at me from the window of their van (and yes, it was white).

I rode past the Sally Army building on the High Street and past the Anchor (boarded up for two years now) then through the Edgelands where the superstores loomed, then across the Sheffield Road and onto the Rotherham Road. The tarmac was fresh and Penelope's wheels sang. I rode past the lake as far as the crossroads with the Worksop Road, then I turned round and came back and had a shower. In all the journey was only three miles, but I felt a little dizzy afterwards and the next day my arse bones ached terribly though I kept this from Beth who was still against the whole thing.

My next few rides were the same, a mile or so around town. After a week of such pootling I tried a twelve mile loop out to Kiveton and back. This was hardly any distance really and I wouldn't have even broken sweat in my younger days, but it was enough for me now, especially as it involved a draining climb up the dreaded hill on Packman Lane on the return leg.

Packman Lane was an ancient, single-track road, bordered on either side by rolling fields across which a patient, restless wind endlessly scoured. From the end of it you could see the road curving and rising in front of you, towards the dark mass of Loscar Wood on the horizon, around which the road curved like a loving arm. Looking around you'd never guess there were major towns just a few miles away. It was a timeless place, and I felt at one with things as I cycled along Packman Lane, readying myself for the ascent.

The hill was long and increased in gradient as you reached the summit, so you had to pace yourself, select the right gear, so that you had the legs to make it all the way to the top. Ten, twenty years ago I would have flown up it on the big ring, but now I ground painfully up it in the granny gear, mashing the pedals and panting and sweating with exertion. As I struggled, another cyclist passed me at speed and startled me a bit. He shouted something over his shoulder as he sped away but I couldn't make out what and I watched him recede into the distance with a sullen sense of envy. I told myself not to be so silly. This guy was clearly a pro, with a brand new bike, clipless pedals (not that I would ever bother), the build of a fit whippet and thousands of miles under his wheels. I was unfit, overweight, recovering from a heart attack; I was bound to be overtaken by other cyclists, and not just pros like this guy – probably everyone could lap me. But the race is not with others, it is with yourself; I would measure my own performance and chart the improvement as the weeks progressed, and soon, I was sure, I would be able to challenge this rider on Packman Hill and even, one triumphant day, overtake the bastard.

Full of such thoughts I wheezed my way to the top of the hill. I felt drained of energy and my legs felt as if they had been hollowed out and filled with water. But after five minutes rest to enjoy the view I was back in the saddle and zooming down the other side of the hill, then home for a shower and some tea. Beth seemed relieved and reassured by the healthy glow on my wind-chapped cheeks.

I didn't let on about the tingling and numbness in my hands and feet, but that was probably down to poor circulation, and would go away as I got fitter.

It was great to be back in the saddle. I have always loved cycling, the feeling of freedom, the sense of adventure, even danger at times. If you are fit enough cycling becomes effortless and the sensation is the nearest you can get to flying. I wasn't fit enough, not yet, but with Penelope's help I would be again, and I resolved to cycle this twelve mile route three times a week, then once a day, until I could do it without breaking sweat, zooming down the hills, spinning up the hills, all with that indefinable, ineffable joy that riding a well maintained machine gives you.

The weird thing was, I seemed to encounter this other rider almost every time I rode that route, and always on Packman Hill, near the top at Loscar Wood. His frame was white and his wheels red, and he wore top of the range cycling gear all in red and white; he reminded me of a tube of toothpaste, so I dubbed him Signal Man. I did my rides in the afternoon, starting at about 2 p.m., so he must have been unemployed, or self-employed, or not needing to go to work for some other reason; or maybe out for a lunchtime ride from his work, whatever it was. Every time he would pass me without warning (doubt he even had a bell), whisking past as if he had just materialised behind me; but of course he must have been approaching me all along Packman Lane, watching and maybe laughing at my sluggish progress, advancing inexorably and silently towards me, and then taking me in a sudden surge of acceleration as the road curled around Loscar Wood.

I tried looking back as I advanced along Packman Lane but I never spotted him. He always took me on the curve around Loscar Wood, where I couldn't see him approach, like he was playing a game. Showing off. Well in all that gear he looked like he was a bit of a poser.

And when he passed me he'd always call back over his shoulder. Words of encouragement? Or derision? I could never make them out. I told Beth about him, thinking she might know him, and she told me that he was probably the ghost of a dead cyclist crushed by an artic on the Sheffield Road, endlessly riding the same route again and again, a lycra-clad Flying Dutchman of the Derbyshire dales.

How I wish she'd never told me that. Not after what happened.

It was about a month into my new fitness regime. I was progressing well, the twelve mile route now taking me fifty minutes where once it had taken two hours. Packman Hill was less gruelling, and I didn't need the granny gear any more. The cardiologist was pleased and Beth had now accepted that my affair with Penelope was back on. All was well.

The only fly in the ointment was Signal Man.

Was he stalking me? If so, why? Why target a middle aged, fat, balding old sod like me? And what was it he kept shouting at me?

Or was it some sort of obscure game?

One Sunday in mid-October I resolved to find out. I'd worked out that on Saturdays I never encountered him, only during the week and sometimes on a Sunday. So one Sunday I set off at two, as usual, and rode the usual twelve-mile route. I took it slowly up Packman Hill, anticipating at any moment – and then there he was, passing me in a flash of red and white and spinning legs and the usual shouted words.

"Hey, mate!" I called after him. "Stop! Wait a sec – I want to talk to you!"

He must have heard me, but paid me no heed, and sailed off down the hill back towards Clowne.

Bugger! Different tactics were called for.

The very next day, a Monday, I set off for my usual ride but started earlier, about half one. And when I got to the top of Packman Hill, I stopped and looked back. The road was clear, a grey thread between the ploughed fields. A wind had picked up and the trees in Loscar Wood were dancing as if trying to throw off their leaves.

Then, I saw him, a distant but distinct dot between the trees in the distance.

I stood waiting for him in the middle of the road, watching him approach, blocking the way with Penelope, forcing him to stop.

He braked, unclipped and dismounted, and stood holding his bike. Beneath the helmet was a thin, smirking, hawk-like face, on top of a slim, toned body. Blue eyes regarded me with a look of amusement beneath sandy brows.

We stood in silence facing each other, the only sound the rustling of the wind in the trees.

"Well?" he said.

"Well," I replied. "I can't help but notice you've been overtaking me on this hill most days for the past month."

"So?"

"It's not that I mind," I went on. "I just want to know what the hell it is you've been shouting at me!"

At this he threw his head back and laughed. "You don't want to know!"

"I do want to know, you – I just want to know!" I felt myself getting hot, despite the coolness of the day.

"It's not complimentary."

"I bet it isn't."

"Look, let me get past, will you?"

"Buggered up your timings, have I?"

He frowned at me, and moved to get back onto his bike. Then he seemed to reconsider. "What would you know, you fat bastard? No wonder your bike needs those chunky fucking tyres, you lardo! Call yourself a serious cyclist? You look old, but you're surely a total noob, you've not even aligned the tyre logos with your valves! And look at that chain! How much oil have you spunked over that? Ever heard of GT-85? And that saddle! Fucking hell, doesn't the horse want that back? And your pedals – MTB, I can hardly believe my fucking eyes!

Clipless, for God's sake! Clipless! I bet you mash those fuckers like a pig on a treadmill, with those – what are they, clogs?! No wonder you're struggling up this little bump in the road, fatty, that old boneshaker must weigh a ton. And pale blue? What is it, a girl's bike? Jesus! What a pile of shit! Can't you afford a proper grown up one?"

I felt as if a big fist had closed around my head. There was a roaring in my ears. I felt at once completely calm, yet my skin felt pierced by a million needles of fire. I picked up Penelope by saddle and handlebars, and brought her down on top of Signal Man's head. The impact jarred my arms and I dropped Penelope. Signal Man went down and his cracked helmet fell away and rolled to one side. His legs got tangled in his bike and he sprawled on the tarmac.

I felt as if I was being controlled by someone, something else. I picked up Penelope and walked over to Signal Man. He was on his back, face twisted in pain and anger, spittle foaming his lips. Angry eyes met mine and he started to get back up. Quickly I pressed Penelope's front wheel onto his throat and pushed down, hard, putting all my weight on the handlebars. He began to make the most awful gurgling, choking sound, so I pressed harder. He looked at me with a pleading expression, and tears streamed from his eyes. I banged Penelope's front wheel down hard on his throat again but I slipped and almost fell. Signal Man managed to twist away from me and get on all fours. I stepped after him and stamped on his back, sending him sprawling. I had to finish this, in case some traffic came along.

I had to finish this quick.

So I smashed the back of his head in with Penelope's chainring. There was a sharp, cracking, crunching sound as the sharp metal teeth bit into his skull. Dark blood began to surge into his sandy hair. Signal Man uttered a roaring scream so I ground the chainring down and down again and again until the back of his head was a mass of hair and blood and mushy brain matter and splinters of bone, sharp and white amidst the mess. His final breath came as a long throaty hiss. His body jerked and shuddered for a while, as if he was being electrocuted, and then he was still. Blood pooled around his carcass like spilled oil.

I walked Penelope to the five-bar gate on the side of the road and leaned her there. I was still calm, though now I felt cold and it was like I was looking down on myself from far above.

"Sorry about that, old girl," I said to Penelope, patting her saddle. She would never tell. She was the only one I could ever trust.

I dragged Signal Man into Loscar Wood, in the midst of which was a dark, deep pond. Into that he went, as did his bike (shame, it was a bloody good model), and his helmet. I used my bottle to fetch water to wash the blood away from the road, then cleaned myself up as best I could, and then cycled home. I chucked all my gear, even the gloves, in the washing machine, had a shower and then made a cup of tea.

I sat in the living room for an hour staring at nothing, my mind feeling curiously empty. Then I turned on the telly and selected BBC News. Would it have been reported yet? No, the body won't be found for days, weeks. Months. Perhaps not ever.

I might even get away with it.

I sat for another hour not listening to the news. I snapped out of my trance when I realised my hands were shaking. I held them up to my face, stared at them as if I'd never seen them before.

That was when Beth came home from work. She found me zonked on the sofa.

"Are you all right?"

"Yes... been out for another ride. The usual route."

I could see him in my mind, the pleading eyes, the cracked egg of his bloodied head.

Beth smiled, then frowned. "Are you okay? You look done in."

"Yeah." I tried to smile. It must have looked ghastly. "I am a bit. Think I'll give Penelope a rest for a week or two."

***

There was a bit of a hoo-ha over a missing cyclist, but they never found the body. That was six months ago and I'm riding almost every day now. Twenty, thirty, even fifty miles. I'm losing weight fast and feeling fitter, stronger. So any bastard that cuts me up or pisses me off now better watch out. It can be murder out there on these lonely roads.

Poo the Winged Serpent
by Richard Freeman

There is a very special lady in my life. She's not like other gals. For starters she's 84-years-old but she's still a looker. She was a record holder for eleven months. Oh yes and she's 1049 feet tall. The lady in my life is the Chrysler building, the most beautiful skyscraper in the whole wide world.

Sure the Empire State Building is taller. It robbed my baby of her title of the world's tallest building in 1931, less than a year after the Chrysler Building was completed. But I always say, *"What the hell, the Chrysler Building is far better looking."*

Let's face it; the Empire State Building has only one claim to fame, it had an outsized gorilla fall off it in the 1930s. Big friggin deal. The Chrysler Building had something much meaner than a big monkey.

Anyhow I'd better introduce myself. I'm Mike Kowalski and I'm the janitor at the Chrysler Building. To be more precise I'm the head janitor. There are over fifty of us. After all, when you have 77 storeys and hundreds of rooms one guy can't cover them all. But I'm the head honcho of janitors and if there is any mess, the buck stops with me. Oh boy, has there been some mess on that building!

You would have had to be living in a cave on Mars not to have heard all about the freaky events of October 1982 that centred around my lovely lady. But I'll wager you've not heard it from one of the insiders. Oh, you will have seen the news reports and heard the breathless voiceovers. You will have read the front pages of the national rags with the scary photos. You may have even watched one of the umpteen documentaries made about it, but I want to tell you my story. I had to clean the damn thing up after all!

October 1st 1982 the shit really hit the fan, or rather the shit hit the pavement. We didn't know what it was at first, only that it was a bloody great mess and it stank like a dozen open graves. It was splattered all over the pavement on 42nd Street. They would not have wanted this in that musical I can tell you.

The stuff was a huge mass of yellowy-white and greeny-brown matter. The greenish stuff was solid and the white stuff was semi-liquid. It had the consistency of one of those thick shakes they serve at McDonalds and it looked about as appetizing. The central mass was as big as a car and the liquid splatter covered yards in every direction. It would have killed anyone it hit. Thank god it fell before rush hour and no one was underneath it. It did however spray a number of New York taxies and splashed back over the windows of our lobby and first floor and stuck up the revolving doors.

Mr Remington, the manager went stark raving mad. I can still picture him, red in the face and looking about five seconds away from a cardiac arrest.

"What in the name of sweet Jesus is this?" He bellowed and jumped up and down like a demented jack-in-the-box. "Thank god Mr Kent Cooke ain't here to see this! We gotta get this cleaned up before any of the tenants get here."

Mr Kent Cook was the entrepreneur who owned the Washington Redskins and the Chrysler Building at the time. Thankfully he was on holiday in Canada.

The Chrysler Building was and is mainly used as offices. Some of the tenants were high falutin' law firms like Black Rome and Troutman Sanders. These big shot lawyer types were not going to like wading through foul smelling gunk in their Armani suits and $1000 shoes.

Technically the stuff was on the pavement outside the building and hence the responsibility of the sanitation department but we knew who was going to clear it up. You guessed it, me and the boys. We could have argued but by the time the sanitation depot sent anyone, the workers would be here and all hell would break loose.

At first I thought the stuff might be some weird fungus that grew underground and forced its way up through the pavement. Here in New York you hear all kinds of urban legends, alligators in the sewers, giant rats in the slums, cannibal mutants in the Subway tunnels and all that. But soon it became apparent that the stuff, whatever it was had fallen from the sky, not erupted from under the pavement. We shovelled it into sacks, scrubbed with disinfectant and then hosed down the whole area. The sanitation boys finally did turn up, just as we had finished, lucky stiffs. They took some of the stuff away for analysis.

Mr Remington thought it might have been waste that had fallen from an airplane. New York is one of the busiest cities in the world. Dozens of planes fly right over us every day. Mr R was on the phone all day to the airports finding out which planes had flown over and when. Turns out none of them had been above us when this stuff fell.

Several eye witnesses swore they had seen the gunk fall out of an apparently clear sky.

In the days that followed there was much speculation as to the nature of the stuff and from whence it had come.

Young Timmy O'Tool, one of the bell hops seemed to think it could have been a mass of pigeon shit.

"You ... you see there must be so many pigeons up in the crown, thousands of 'em I'd say, that their droppings all coagulated into one big mass and it got too heavy and fell off the side!"

"No way Timmy," I said shaking my head, "that stuff, if it is shit, is fresh. For pigeon droppings to form a mass like that they would all be as dry as Phyllis Diller's ..."

Thankfully I never got to finish that sentence. Mr Remington burst in on us as we were having a crafty smoke. He was waving a big brown envelope in his hand.

"The Sanitation depot sent the samples off to the university to have them analysed. The boffins over there say the stuff's excrement!"

"We worked that out for ourselves," I said.

"But there's more," Mr R went on, "the samples seem to contain cells that are partly bird and partly reptile."

We all looked blankly at him.

"You mean like one of them there pre-historic bird things?" said Winston from storage.

"A pterodactyl?" I offered

"Yeo, one of them critters."

"Or maybe there is a flying zoo."

"Look, I've no idea what it is," said Mr R, "but it made an awful mess right outside the foyer and the university has positively identified the mess as droppings."

I shook my head. "So we know its shit but we don't know what made it or where it came from. We're no better off than before."

It was a surreal situation, discussing a giant pile of shit that seemingly came from nowhere.

Next day Eddie from security gets his head busted. He says three guys walked into his office and one whupped him up the side of the head with the butt of a revolver. They got clean away. He says he recognized one of the guys. A weasley looking fella he saw creeping around up on the 71st floor a few days before. The guy gave him the slip, apparently he went up higher. The police didn't give two hoots they have bigger fish to fry. Security in the Chrysler Building was a joke back then, a handful of guys who were mostly drunks. Eddie was pretty heavily into the sauce and we all thought he had just drunkenly slipped up and banged his head.

After that things quietened down for a few days. Well, at least in my lady. Out in the Big Apple some weird stuff was happening. The NYCPD had their hands full. The papers were bursting with stories about murders and disappearances. Corpses were turning up that had been literally skinned. The bodies had been found in hotel rooms, warehouses, rivers, you name it. The cops were chasing some sort of cult angle and were bringing in anthropologists and experts in the occult. At the same time people were vanishing. The odd thing was that they were all vanishing from the tops of tall buildings. People disappeared from penthouse swimming pools, construction workers on high rise apartment blocks. They weren't falling off, no bodies were ever found. Back then the police were treating the murders and the vanishings as separate cases. We know better now.

Anyhow after a week or so we get a complaint from one of our tenants. Troutman Sanders complained about white paint all over the windows of their offices up on the 71st floor. The 71st is the last occupied floor. The six floors above that are the insides of the 'crown' that wonderful art deco sunburst that sits atop my lady. It's just for ornamentation, like a rich dame's fine hat.

I took an elevator up and had a peek myself. It was true; thick white gunk was splattered all across the windows. It ruined a lovely view. I had a feeling that this was not paint though. It looked like that crap we had to clear up a few days before. I told them I would get right on the case. They wanted to know if there was repair work being done on the floors above them because it had got a bit noisy there in recent days, apparently with a lot of bumping and dragging. They figured some workmen had knocked over a bunch of paint cans. No work had been done on the crown for years.

The Chrysler building is so tall that you can't see the top from street level. So on my dinner hour, I take my packed lunch down to Ralph Bunche Park and had a gander at the crown from a distance. As sure as apples is apples there were big white streaks running down the crown. It looked like bird crap but on a huge scale. A thought had started to form in my head back then but I dismissed it as crackers. Turns out I was not crackers at all.

Mr R wanted me and the boys to clean up Troutman Sanders' windows but we said no. I really put my foot down on this one. Cleaning giant crap off the pavement is one thing. Cleaning it off windows the best part of a thousand feet up is another kettle of fish.

"Look Mr R," I says, "look, we are contracted to clean the inside of the building, not the outside. We ain't got no insurance to cover that."

So they bring in some window cleaners from a firm that specialises in skyscrapers. Those guys had some balls I'll tell ya. You wouldn't get me on a bench dangling from a couple of ropes that far up. So the guys clean up the gunk good and proper. Troutman Sanders are pleased, Mr R is pleased, I'm pleased me and the boy's didn't have to do it. But the cleaning guys vanished. Their cradle was left up there but there was no sign of them.

Mr R figured that they had got lost somewhere up in the crown. He gives me a flashlight and sends me up 'cos I'm the Chrysler Building dogsbody.

Now, I hadn't been up in the crown for several years. As I said it's not in use so there is little cause to go up there at all. The elevator doesn't come up into the crown so I had to climb the stairs. I looked around all the floors but I found no signs of any window cleaners. Apparently this was where the guy Eddie saw was heading to. The crown was in a pretty poor state of repair. A number of the windows were out and the wind whistled through them. There's always wind at this height and up here it sounded like a weird kind of music, piping round the crown. It should have been cold all the way up there but it felt strangely hot.

The last floor is a kind of big dome underneath the needle. You have to climb up a metal ladder and open a hatch to get access. I climbed up and pushed the hatch aside. Peering in, I saw that part of the dome had fallen in. Most of the space inside was taken up by a gigantic nest. Coiled up on the nest was this, this ... dragon ... serpent ... bird ... thing!

You have seen the photos, the film footage, but none of that does justice to the creature. I saw it in the flesh. A good hundred-and-fifty-feet long, covered in olive green scales. It had four legs with eagle-like talons and a long tail. Its wings were ribbed like a bat's but the skin in-between had elongated scales like feathers that gave them a sort of ragged edge. The thing had them folded over its back but the wingspan must have equalled the thing's length. It had a long neck like a sort of giant scaly swan and a huge, murderous beak. That beak looked as sharp as a guillotine and strong enough to bite a Cadillac clean in two. It had dark, beady eyes that suddenly turned on me.

The dragon-thing let out the most hideous noise. A sort of hissing screech like an old time steam locomotive. I swear I felt all my insides shake with that noise. Then that great snapping beak was coming right at me. I fell back down through the hatch and I heard it clang as the beak snapped at it. Thankfully the monster's head was too large to get through. I don't mind telling you I pissed my pants. That big monkey that climbed up the Empire State had nothing on this beast. It would have kicked his hairy ass.

It was obvious where the missing people had been going, right down the gullet of this winged serpent.

Mr Remington thinks I'm a loony tune. I'm standing in his office shaking like a shitting dog and telling him that the masses of crap that have been falling out of the sky and streaking the building are from a dragon that is nesting in the crown.

"But boss, you said yourself them University Poindexters found a mix of bird and reptile DNA in the crap. If you don't believe me go and look yourself."

Amazingly he did. He told me he was going up to disprove my story and that all I had seen was a big bird, maybe an eagle that had escaped from Central Park Zoo. When he came back down again he was as white as a sheet and had a big wet patch on his pants.

It was at that point an army of cops armed with machine guns came bursting into the lobby and headed for the elevators. They were tooled up like a small army. Magazines of armour piercing and explosive bullets and tracers. They had a skinny, shifty looking guy with them who looked none too pleased to be there. We found out later that this was the guy Eddie had seen creeping around near the crown. Turns out he was some small time jewel thief who had been hiding from some hoods by sneaking up to the top of the building. He found the nest and later tricked the pair of them hoods into going up there and they got wasted by the winged serpent. He had apparently been holding the city to ransom and demanding one million bucks to show the cops where the monster was holed up.

They go right up to the dome under the needle and find the nest is empty save for an egg the size of a three-piece-suite. They turn it into the biggest omelette in the world with a hundred or so bullets post-haste. But then the adult comes back and it's pissed.

For the next half an hour there is a battle above the streets of New York. The serpent comes swooping in to grab cops in its monster beak or send them tumbling down to create meat starfishes on the pavement. The cops keep pumping round after round of armour-piercing bullets into the beast as it flaps around the crown. They must have riddled it with thousands of bullets.

Then suddenly the monster lets out a deafening screech and it crashes down onto the roof of another building across the street, flaps crazily for a while then comes crashing down to the ground right in front of our lobby; one-hundred-and-fifty-feet of lizard-bird tipping the scales at a hundred tons plus, slap bang outside of reception.

If you have been told that the bullets killed the monster it's bullshit. Machine guns are like peashooters to that thing. No the truth is a whole lot weirder.

Remember those ritual murders I told you about? Well it turns out that there is this group of crazy Mexican cultists in town. They have been skinning willing human victims alive (well at first) in sacrifice to Quetzalcoatl (try saying that over a few beers) a giant, flying, Aztec serpent god. These freaks literally prayed the monster back into existence. But when the cops wasted the cult members there was no more worship and the force keeping the god alive was snuffed out. Weird, seems we have the power over gods not visa-versa. Some of the newspaper reports said that one of the detectives on the case thought that once these dragon things lived all over the world but they died out or became 'dormant' when the cults that worshiped them, and made human sacrifices to them stopped their veneration. His words not mine, hell I'm only a janitor.

Guess who had to clean up a dead dragon from off of 42nd street? Yes ol' muggins Mike Kowalski. You can see the damn thing stuffed at Smithsonian, still gives me the shivers.

Anyhow, all that happened 32 years ago. Its 2014, I'm nearing retirement age now. Thankfully nothing remotely like that has ever happened again. Giant Aztec dragon gods are one thing I can do without.

Now what the hell is all the commotion going on outside? Can't a guy have a nice cup of Joe and a baloney sandwich in peace? Sounds like some sort of earth tremor. We don't usually get those here on the east coast. I'll take a gander out the window. Lots of people running and screaming. What's that stomping down 42nd street crushing cabs and buses? It looks like a 350-foot tall mutant Tyrannosaurus rex from Japan and what's more, it's breathing radioactive fire! I gotta get out of this business. I'm too old for this shit!

edited by Stephanie Ellis & S.G. Mulholland

A Stitch in Frankenstein Saves Nine
by Stewart Hotston

The room smelt empty and sick. The doctor, an old woman by the name of Moore, had shunted the family out; they were worrying at the young man in the bed whose heart was failing him. The last thing he needed was their anxiety eating at him.

"Adrian, the operation has its risks," she said to him. He looked at her with cynical eyes. "It's still your only chance for a normal life."

"My mum said you're the best in the world." He said it as an accusation, a charge against the idea that the surgery may not be successful.

"I've no idea who the best is. I'm certainly experienced. If it can be done then I'm well placed to make that happen." She checked the door was shut. "I've a story to tell you, about why I think you should choose the operation. About why it's even possible. Can I tell you?"

Adrian nodded, so she sat herself down and began.

***

My story starts some sixty years earlier, with a careworn looking medic staring at a patchwork man stood in his surgery.

"I remember when you first came in," said Humbert. He held the severed arm in his hands, looking at it first this way then that. It was missing the thumb, the middle finger, while the elbow was flayed badly enough to show the bone like a china cast. "I'm sure there's an interesting tale behind this particular injury."

His patient, a slightly pallid man with slick black hair and an uncannily square jaw, rested his other elbow on his knee and said nothing.

"There's no point being gloomy about it Frank, there's nothing you can do, they all wear out eventually."

Frank looked up from contemplating the scuffs on his slip-on shoes. "It's not like it was wearing out, doctor." He pursed his lips. "The war's over and I wasn't looking to worry about accidental injuries. I'm not about to head off to the Korean peninsula for what's brewing there."

Humbert nodded his agreement, "I understand Frank, I really do. It's not like you could fit in over there anyway." He swung the end of the arm in a gesture that encompassed Frank's form. "You're far too tall and your features too European for anyone to mistake you for a native. You'd attract far too much attention."

"Time was I could find the parts I needed on battlefields or in ruined ghettos." He sighed heavily, echoes of the slaughter of innocents sounding as bittersweet memories.

"It wasn't all fun," said the doctor. "Central Europe was a dog's dinner and you were nearly the main course more than once." Frank shrugged indifferently. "I remember finding you without any legs in Marseille. Some drunken sailors with too much literacy for their own good worked out who you were - remember?"

Frank snorted with mirth, he sounded like a hedgehog snuffling at a cat flap. "One of them had read about the good doctor. Thought he knew what should be done." He sighed sadly, "the sailor obviously didn't take the message as Shelley meant to convey it."

"There's nothing you can do about that my old son," said Humbert. "People will choose what to believe from moment to moment, there are very few of them who hold consistently to their beliefs."

"Why is that?" asked Frank sincerely.

"Because it would mean they'd have to address new situations as grown men and women, to respond with maturity and grace. God forbid Frank, it would demand they act like Christ and most of them are far too happy with him being a distant figure for them to pin their prejudices on. The fewer real demands on their souls religion makes the happier they are."

Frank fixed Humbert with his better eye, a clear blue orb taken from a young girl who died before her time. "I never figured you for a religious man, doctor."

Humbert sat down on a high metal stool next to his examination table. He slowly extracted a high-tar cigarette and lit it with a match. He took a long slow drag before looking at the lit end as if it were a bug under a microscope. "No rational man can exclude the possibility that all this," and he waved his fag around the room, "is nothing more than the surface of things. Materialism assumes that we, the bags of meat we are, have the wherewithal to plumb the depths of creation. The rest of us acknowledge that we're radically incomplete."

Frank waited for him to say more. Instead the doctor stood up, groaning with the effort. He took the severed arm from the operating table with him across the dingy room to sling into a large plastic bin. "Frank, I'm down to the last right arm in my collection. It is, of course, solely for your use, but after this? I'm getting old son, mortality is my lot. After the carnage of the last six years I'm not going to resist any longer than I feel is decent. Oblivion holds a certain attraction after you've witnessed the power of the atom in man's own hands." He thrust his cigarette in Frank's direction, "You are, whether anyone outside of my head realises it, where they're headed. The Avery-MacCleod-McCarty experiment will inevitably lead to the correct structure for DNA being finalised. The good doctor was so far ahead of his time, but yours is coming, like a locomotive crossing a continent. My hope for you, Frank, is that one day you'll be recognised for the miracle you are. The number of breakthroughs you represent are beyond counting."

Frank shook his head, "I've no interest in being someone's miracle, Doctor." He touched the bandaged wound where his arm had previously been attached. "I'd settle for being able to live quietly without interruption, to be able to go to the theatre, to visit the picture house or the dancehall without some joe mistaking me for a communist and picking a fight. I'd settle for my dreams being my own."

"Are you still dreaming of combat?" asked Humbert seriously, approaching Frank and pulling his hair this way and that. Along the man's hairline were seams of neat stitching. Humbert sighed with satisfaction at his handiwork and was comforted that there were no signs of infection; not that he had expected there to be any. Frank never got sick, never rejected the organs or limbs attached to him, and apparently couldn't suffer nerve damage except from what pre-existed an item's attachment to him.

"I am. I've died countless times," said Frank. The doctor shone a light into his eyes, left then right. "Each time it's painful, excruciating. There's no escape and no respite. God have mercy."

"You know," said Humbert, taking Frank's temperature by shoving a thermometer under his arm, "it's said that if you died in your dreams you would truly die."

Frank snorted loud and hard. "What dreams may come eh?" Humbert laughed wryly at Frank's allusion while the big man continued speaking. "Doctor, this brain has been with me for thirteen years and the gent it belonged to before me was a bookish man. I sometimes wonder how he managed to find a wife, have five children, write poetry and fight in a war before he caught a landmine in northern Italy. He still dreams of loving his wife, of the explosion which killed him." He frowned. "I'm not sure all the dreams are his."

"The memory resides in brain matter," said Humbert firmly. "The only dreams you can have are yours and his."

"Then he was also given to wearing dresses and lived with his parents who gave him a wooden doll for Christmas before he died."

Humbert coughed to hide his surprise, "You've not mentioned this before."

"I've tried not to dwell on it," said Frank.

The doctor thought about it for a few moments, "Your gut, where did that come from?"

"A woman. Auxiliary, a firefighter in Paris. Died in a car accident, run over by her own fire engine while trying to divert the rescued to the paramedics."

"It's possible her enteric nervous system is communicating with your central nervous system. Honestly, I'm guessing. The science is beyond me."

Frank shrugged, waving away a coil of cigarette smoke from his face. "It's ok, Doctor, I came to a peace about who I am a long time ago. The downsides are inescapable and one has to accept them or risk becoming bedridden with melancholy."

Humbert pulled a large file out of a safe under his desk. The folder was barely uniform, with paper of all colours and sizes spilling out from a central cord which was laced through each piece. He put the folder on the desk, opening it with a reverence that bordered the holy. "I'm too old for this now, Frank. I have to give this back to you."

Frank sighed and tried to smile, "I understand. I guess you must be sixty-eight now?"

Humbert nodded, "I am. I served my country through the two wars and all that time I have tried my best to be the friend you have needed. In that time we've discovered DNA, penicillin has become common place and a world of medical promise has been opened up before us because of it. I have read the good doctor's notes a dozen times and admit I am still like a child stood in awe before medicine's *Tractatus Logico-Philosophicus*."

"You have done more for me that I could ever have asked," said Frank sincerely.

"You're ninety now, Frank. I hope that you have many decades of life before you. I hope that you can still find happiness."

"Life is like walking up a mountain - you should pace yourself and concentrate on putting one foot in front of the other," said Frank quietly.

"At least the views are good," said Humbert wryly.

Frank laughed for the first time since he'd arrived, he sounded like a rumbling wagon. "Aye. True enough."

Humbert put the manuscript in Frank's hands, "You need this. I've added my own notes, case history as well as three names of those younger than myself who you should be able to trust. I'd start with Beatrix Moore, a niece of a friend of mine. We worked the Somme together. We both dream of faces in the mud asking for our help."

The doctor was finished with his examination, "You're in as rude health as I've known you Frank, I can have the new arm attached in about three hours. Do you want a sedative to help pass the time?"

Frank transferred himself to the operating table, slowly undressing as he sat on the surface, like Humpty Dumpty voluntary removing his own shell. When he was done, Frank lay back slowly and closed his eyes. "Time is all I have Doctor. Feel free to take as much as you want."

"Why so melancholy?" asked Humbert sadly.

Frank took the proffered gas and sank willingly into a dreamless slumber without answering.

***

The sign said Dr. B. Moore. It was brass, polished and obviously new. Frank was impressed; Humbert had practised in the army whenever the opportunity allowed, and if it didn't he was found in back alleys, in people's living rooms. Humbert did the operations others wouldn't.

He rang the buzzer, looking around him as he did so. It was seven am on a Saturday morning, the time suggested to him by Dr Moore. The street of red brick town houses was sleepy and silent. He'd left Manhattan at half five, but even then the place was crazy with workers leaving for new shifts, others blearily returning home together with the entertained finding their way back from the long Friday night blitz. So many people in one place made Frank nervous, it wasn't easy to escape notice among a crowd and there was always one who thought it would be fine to point out the giant with the odd features trying to make his way quietly along the street. Frank had once been angry enough in his own self to think nothing of crushing a man's skull for forcing him to stand his ground. That fury had drained out of him in the first Great War, leaving an emptiness he recognised as Nietzsche's abyss. He was grateful for Dr Moore's intuitive sensitivity in asking him to come so early on Saturday morning.

The door opened in one single movement. A small plump woman in a loam coloured tweed skirt suit and thin black glasses stood on the other side. "Good morning!" she said happily and stood back to let him enter. Frank stepped across the threshold, taking his trilby off as he did so. "You are most welcome, Mr. Sohn. Please, please follow me."

Frank assumed it was Doctor Moore herself and moved after her. She showed him into a comfortably-furnished drawing room. The furniture was dark hard wood, probably from the Old World; he had seen the inside of enough houses in the old country to know wealth when he saw it. He found a stool, missing its piano, and sat down gingerly on the worn green velvet, clutching his hat in his hands.

"Let me take your coat and hat," said Dr Moore.

Frank looked around the room after she had left with his things. She had a new telephone, a wireless on the desk. The shelves were full of books with titles that reminded him of Humbert. A copy of Shelley's story was carefully placed so he could read the cover from where he sat. She clearly wanted him to know she knew but what else was she trying to tell him? He'd lived long enough to know that people always meant more than they initially thought when they communicated. From the book's prominence he guessed she wanted him to be comforted, reassured. Possibly she wanted him to feel vulnerable too; the book showed that she knew who he was.

"I'm so glad you could make it. Doctor Handelblatt was very fond of you."

"How did you meet?" asked Frank.

She sat on a long leather recliner under the window, "At a conference at the end of the war. We were trying to decide on how the research the Nazis had been undertaking should be treated." She wrung her hands. "As you might imagine, there is a great deal of sensitivity about how and why they did what they did, but the results. Well, the results are still years ahead of where our own lines of research were taking us."

Frank sat there listening to her talk. It was his interview as much as it was hers. "I was one of the few researchers who felt the outcomes could be used to redeem the horrors that were their genesis. Doctor Handelblatt was a refugee who agreed with me. Did he ever tell you about the liberation of Dachau? I was here at home but he was there. His story moved me in such a way that I knew we shared an understanding about the redemption of horror."

Frank didn't want her to know that he too, had been there.

Doctor Moore watched the expressions passing over his face and slowed to a stop. Collecting herself she asked, "How can I help you?"

"Was the doctor not clear?" asked Frank, suddenly nervous that she did not really know his needs.

She shook her head. "He said that you would be the best person to tell me."

Frank stared at her, his eyes wide enough to make her wonder if they might fall out. She desperately wanted to ask him if his creator was as Shelley described him; the hubris and the hope, the madness and tragedy. She held her tongue - the very fact of Frank's presence here in her office meant Shelley hadn't told the whole truth. If Beatrix knew one thing it was that life was infinitely more banal than the heart could wish for.

"I'm like an old car, Doctor," said Frank. "My parts wear out and need replacing. The doctor was compassionate towards me. He would help me like a mechanic would see to a car that needed a new camshaft."

"Ok," said Moore slowly. No wonder Humbert always edged round the issue when they had talked about Frank's case history. "And who would order the parts?"

Frank actually laughed, his face crinkling with pleasure. "If we follow this to its end? We both did, we spent much of our time together in the wars." He shrugged, "It was easier then."

"You're a veteran?" she asked, impressed that he would have fought at all, given his condition.

"Of course. In the first it was, in the cold light of day, because I was still angry."

Beatrix couldn't help herself, "You were angry?"

Frank's eyes glanced at the book on her desk, "I burned like the sun, setting fire to everything and everyone that came near. It was a dangerous time, full of angels and demons. I was at home among them." Dr. Moore felt fear transfix her at his words. "Europe remains a place of unequalled horror for me as well. My anger is buried in the trenches with men who, in the end, I had no choice but to rely on. Friendship is too small a word for what was asked of them there. If you'll forgive me stretching the metaphor, it was easy for me to find parts when I was living in a scrap yard."

"You met Dr. Handelblatt in the second war?" asked Moore.

"No, we met in the first, but not in theatre. In the second we signed up together. Despite my attempts the British army insisted that I was a perfect candidate for the resistance."

"You were in France then."

"Occasionally. When they said resistance they meant all of them. I speak most of Europe's main languages to some degree, and I was hardly likely to be mistaken for an Aryan. The doctor was also asked to work behind enemy lines. We were fortunate; it allowed us to stay in contact, probably more so than if we had been regular joes."

"What are you willing to do now? You know, to get your spare parts?" asked Moore and saw fear in his eyes for the first time.

"I can pay and I can work. I've worked in many morgues and with many morticians. I would rather not rob graves nor could I accept bodies from the mob. I have no problem with parts that have a criminal origin, except for stomachs and brains."

"Why not stomachs?" said the doctor.

"Bleed through. The stomach is a bag of nerves that have a life of their own. Like they do with the brain, people's memories and desires reach out to me with long fingers and sweet words," said Frank. "It's taken me a long time to find out the person I want to be; to understand the difference between what I want to be and the inclinations that are mine in being embodied. Other people's contributions to my identity should really be my choice. No criminals, murderers or those who take pleasure in the pain of others."

"What if you had no choice?" asked Moore, trying to set a base line.

"You mean would I die rather than compromise? Of course not. However, I fervently pray I shall never have to make that choice," said Frank.

"Let's hope that we don't have to rely on God," said Moore, smiling.

Frank didn't reply but realised the woman had never seen a trench, never cleared out a liquidation room. He realised then that she didn't understand Shelley's book. He wanted to ask her if she thought he was a monster, he guessed it was taking her entire sense of professionalism not to ask him about the professor. He appreciated all this but hoped there was more to her than being a fine doctor. He trusted Humbert; it was to remember him that he had come here in the first place. Dr. Moore was still an unknown to him and, unless they found a job to do together, would always be less than the partnership of Handelblatt and Sohn.

Frank pulled a small gold ingot from his trouser pocket. He watched Moore's response very carefully. "I can pay my way," he said and held out the two ounce bar in the palm of his hand.

Moore rocked back on her seat and stammered.

"It's mine legitimately," he said quickly putting it on the table as if it were an insect about to bite him.

"It's not money I see as being the problem Mr Sohn," said Moore hesitantly. "I'm sure you've worked out how to pass ports and borders." She turned toward the gold. "Money buys most things in the United States. However, you have indicated no interest in pursuing the most obvious options for obtaining parts for your car. If we are to come to some arrangement the most difficult question before us is the one of spares." She took off her glasses and used an arm of the frame to push the gold in his direction. "Take that until we have need for it."

They couldn't find common ground. Moore could, or would, offer him no ideas and he, a new baby in the arms of Lady Liberty didn't even know what was possible. Frank left Moore's office in a deep funk. The next few months passed without incident, with the opening up of the first freeways he had the blessed opportunity to drive alone, without the pressure of human contact. He loved conversation, loved discussing what he heard, saw and read but it was hard finding communities where someone wouldn't seek to set him up as their outsider over whatever infraction they deemed marked him alien. America, friend to the idea of the immigrant was harsh to the actual individuals who made up that heaving pulp of flesh and hope. He decided not to visit the other prospects Handelblatt had provided him. Instead he concentrated on seeing as much of the USA and Canada as he could fit in.

Spring turned to summer. The nails began to fall off his left hand, hair sprouted in thick angular clumps. Frank sat on the beach in Chicago one afternoon, plucking the unsightly growths one by one, and contemplated his future as cargo ships darkened the horizon of Lake Michigan.

The book the doctor had given him remained hidden under the driver's seat of his articulated lorry. Frank was an accomplished autodidact but medicine was so much Latin and alchemy to him. He loved the idea of genetics but couldn't see how it would help a mongrel like him. A week later the little finger turned blue, then purple. When it went numb he knew he could put off a return visit to Dr Moore no longer.

Beatrix had given him her direct number to ring out of hours. "My secretary isn't necessary for us to meet," she had said.

She sounded surprised to hear from him. "Mr Sohn. How are you? I thought that when you didn't contact me after a month…" She left the end of her sentence unsaid.

Frank shrugged on his end of the receiver. "Time is no respecter of men's decisions." Doctor Moore collected herself and they arranged a time for him to visit. Normally he would have waited, his driving meant he was hundreds of miles away, but the purple colour was starting to spread in a way that he knew needed seeing to.

Three days later he was stood on the edge of her borough, evening heat hazing his view down the street, the smell of softened tarmac in the air. The truck had been left in Brooklyn and he'd caught the metro to her address. The twelve foot high cabin was simply too conspicuous in this well to do neighbourhood.

Her office was as he remembered it. Shelley was nowhere to be seen.

"What happened?" she asked once they were settled. He held out his hand. Doctor Moore examined it slowly. When she was done she asked if it hurt and how long it had been developing. "Some form of cell death." She looked up at him as if he were a collaborator, "I'm guessing you've seen this before?"

Frank felt vulnerable, as if, without his permission, she was seeing into his soul. It left him tongue-tied. "Yes."

"I have been thinking since we last met," she said, choosing her words deliberately. "I had hoped you would contact me sooner than this. I've had some ideas."

Her comments were unexpected. "Ideas?" he asked.

"Yes, we're just starting to understand that maybe people can use other people's organs." She laughed, a double ha of nervousness. "You obviously know it can be done."

He nodded, but didn't see how that would help. He couldn't register as in need of organs legitimately.

"There's a problem though. The body protects itself from invaders and, nearly always, transplants are seen by the host as a hostile organism. People live for days or weeks before their own systems reject the very thing that's supposed to give them new life. I've recently taken on a residency where I can research these techniques." She sat back in her chair and rested her hands on her knees. Dr. Moore watched Frank.

"You think I can help?" he said slowly.

"You could let us operate on you. We could transplant organs to you and see how you're different to other people." He was about to object, but she held up her hand, "I know, that wouldn't work for you - you only need replacements occasionally and it's not a long-term solution. However, I was wondering, did Doctor Handelblatt ever give you his own notes, or any ... other research?"

The cover of the folder appeared in the front of his mind. He was too frightened of the hope it gave him to answer immediately. Doctor Moore bit her lip, she could see the answer vibrating through his whole body. Frank was faced with the decision he wasn't ready for - whether he trusted Moore with his entire being. In that folder was not just his medical history but the notes the professor had made in creating him. In every sense she would know more about him than he did. He looked down at his finger and considered the alternatives.

"I have a folder. Some of it is the professor's. Some is the doctor's. I can let you see it. It may help you. How will it help me?"

"I think that the notes contain ways the professor discovered to help smooth the acceptance process. I believe they could help me establish a new science and give thousands of people a second chance. It will need trials, I'll need anonymous patients to operate on. We will need to operate on every conceivable part of the body. And it will take time. Lots of time. I'm not young now Mr Sohn. I don't see us mastering this science before I'm too old to work with you any longer."

Frank's face fell. "I mean that the opportunities will continue to arise decades from now. I can't promise anything, even now, but if the professor's genius is what I hope then I will have legitimate access to good organs for the rest of my career."

"You're going to need me to do this?" asked Frank.

Moore nodded, "Yes. At least right now. I'd hope that in a week or so I'd be able to perform my first operation and see about transplanting a finger." She laughed in spite of herself. "It's going to get harder as the years progress. People will want rules, they will want checks and balances. For now we can pioneer, this is the United States after all."

"I'll get the book," said Frank and stood to leave.

"Wait!" said Moore. "I've a request of you." Frank turned to face her, chin on his chest as he looked down. "Humbert was right about you. I hope he was right about me. I won't be here as long as you. I want you to learn medicine. I want you to assist me when I'm not working more directly with you. I want you to learn to write research. If you don't become part of this system now then when I'm no longer of service to you it may be too late for you to find other sources for parts that you will be happy with. The world is changing Frank. The magic is leaving; in its place is coming quantity, measurement and classification."

"I don't know," said Frank. "Everything I've ever learnt I've learnt for myself."

"These ideas aren't my own," said Moore as if trying to get him to listen to the spaces in between the words, "Humbert wrote about this. He wrote about you. To me. Please."

"I'll get the book," said Frank.

***

Adrian listened politely at first but by the end his attention was complete. When Moore finished her tale he immediately asked, "Is that it? What happened to Frank?"

She smiled; no question about its truth, about whether she was the same Moore as in the story, just a yearning for the man he identified with.

"Frank's story is his own. Dr. Moore promised him that she would never reveal the truth about him to anyone." Adrian frowned, "He has given his permission for that part of his story to be retold when I believe it will help others see hope in despair. Besides, after the operation you'll have plenty of time to google the timeline."

Adrian nodded and Beatrix Moore knew then that he would choose the heart transplant operation rather than death.

edited by Stephanie Ellis & S.G. Mulholland

Spyder, Spyder
by David Croser

Is that thing switched on?

Right. Well. Why I murdered Sarah Jane. How the spiders made me confess.

Why I shouldn't be in here.

I'm not mad. Sure, I killed her. Premeditated, cold blood, blah, blah, blah…

But I did it 'cause I wanted her money, her name, all that land, y'know?

Nothing screwy about that. Okay, okay! I know what you're thinking.

I can relate to that. Boy, I shouldn't be 'Detained at Her Majesty's Pleasure'.

I shouldn't be in this hospital. I'm a murderer, sure. Fair cop.

But I'm as sane as you. Okay.

Right. How it happened.

I'm an East Ender. Shoreditch's my manor.

Mannah? Isn't that the word we're supposed to use?

Bollocks. Couldn't wait to get out of that cesspit.

Grew up in this filthy, piss-stained block off Columbia Road.

Druggies in the stairs, screams and arguments you could hear through eggshell walls. Mildewed walls. Christ, it was rotten, my mum's flat.

I mean it. Literally. The whole block was riddled with rot. Dry rot, wet rot, mildew. Hated it. Hated the damp. Hated the thick, ripe stench that clung to everything and everyone. You changed your clothes as often as you could; otherwise you took the smell of the flats with you wherever you went.

"Christ, Miss! Someone open a window. Gavin's gone off again!"

Had to put up with comments like that for years. Hated the damp – and the plants.

Never knew my dad.

Bastard got my ma up the duff and she never saw him again.

Brought me up alone. Struggled hard to make ends meet, just to bring me up.

Wrenches the heartstrings, doesn't it?

Product of a broken home! You can see why he went wrong. Crap.

Ma was a tin-plated selfish bitch.

Soon as I was old enough she'd throw me out. Had to fend for myself most of the time. Number of cold teas, microwave dinners, salads I'd have to make myself. Apart from the salads that is. She'd make them alright.

Veggie, my ma. Loved everything that grew. Flat like frigging greenhouse.

They got the love, the tenderness, the care she had in her.

Some mas like bingo; some have fellas, some its drink – or all three.

Houseplants, my ma.

Told you we lived off Columbia Road. Flower market there of a Sunday.

Guess who's their best customer? Benefit she got for me went on flowers, plants, and window boxes. If she could've shagged the bloody things she would of. And me?

Every May I'd get hay fever and I'd suffer.

God. I'd sound like I'd been smoking sixty-a-day for sixty years, eyes like poached eggs, nose like it was stuffed with iron filings. Ten years I put up with that crap. That's enough about ma.

I left home at sixteen and lived in a squat in Camden while I did my A-Levels.

I had brains, see.

Not for English or History or any of that creative rubbish.

Economics. Business Studies. Modern Languages. Useful stuff.

Lots of people – creative types – say they couldn't give a toss about money.

Look down on anyone that wants to make something of themselves, make a success of their lives. Think the world of business and finance is for plebs.

Not me. It doesn't matter where you're from, what background; you get respect for what you do. A meritocracy. I like that word. And I got that.

Respect.

Started off in a trading house in the City. Small fry to begin with, then I started to build. Buying shares all thought worthless, selling them at just the right time. Made a fortune for the firm. Moved on to futures, currency trading. Those pound signs kept piling up, and the directors started paying me some attention, smiling and slapping me on the back, calling me Guy.

It's not, by the way. Guy, I mean. Gavin Pierce, I was back in Shoreditch, but now it was Guy.

So there I was, one of the highest-grossing dealers in the firm.

By this time I had my choice of the best addresses, down Docklands, in the old East End. There's an irony. And the place! Old warehouse down the West India Dock. Huge open space – bare brick, tiled floors, brushed steel.

I wanted no clutter in there. Clean lines and primary colours. Lots of Conran and Habitat. None of that chintzy crap. No plants either. Another irony.

The warehouse used to be a flower importers!

I had it all. Money. Respect.

But I wasn't one of them.

Not a poof, I mean. One of the old boys.

They respected me, sure – like you respect a pet shark.

But I hadn't gone to none of their schools. I wasn't a member of their clubs.

My daddy wasn't chums with theirs. I might as well have been a gnat at the bottom of Canary Wharf Tower for all the progress I'd made.

Did I envy them?

I'd changed my name. Came from Croydon not Shoreditch if they asked, sure.

But I didn't envy them.

I said I killed Sarah Jane for her money. I did. But I wanted *all* of it.

Let me explain.

I met Sarah Jane at the firm's Christmas ball.

Her dad was Lord Troughton, senior partner.

I'd gone to the ball with Cheryl, this well-fit trader from Futures, but when I saw Sarah Jane I thought – well, why not?

Cheryl knows the score. She and I were good for each other's careers but that's all. Even if there was more I would've slung her for Sarah Jane.

Sarah Jane wasn't a classy dresser.

She had on this red frock, and you could tell that her auburn hair needed a bloody good conditioner. But I didn't care, because of all the women there only she was real. The way she smiled, the way she laughed, and there was nothing forced or calculating about it like everyone else at the do.

We got talking, and would you believe it, we got on really well.

I found Guy's glossy paintwork was wearing away and Gavin was getting to know her. She wasn't a city soul but a country girl. Lord Troughton was old money, had this stately home and thousands of acres down Kent.

Things developed. She liked my wide boy charm, and I began to see more of her – not that her daddy approved. I'd been seeing his daughter for a couple of weeks. It was after work and we were coming out of the board.

The old man clapped a hand on my shoulder.

Seems my daughter's really struck on you, he smiled through clenched teeth, and how would I like to come down for the weekend?

After that it all seemed to move together.

Lady Troughton liked me (thought I was a charming rogue), and before six months was out they were announcing our engagement in *The Times*.

The Troughtons were a traditional lot, so weren't too happy about us moving in together, but their precious daughter's happiness was all that mattered.

I nearly blew it though.

Sarah Jane had moved in while I was at the office.

I'd made sure there was none of Cheryl's stuff lying around (I was still knocking her off), and I'd got Fortnum's to pack the fridge and leave her a soppy box of chocs. Thought I was showing her some consideration.

What I found when I got back was a sodding greenhouse. She'd only brought every sodding houseplant from home with her.

"What are these doing here?! You know how I feel – "

I grabbed a plant and threw it at her.

It missed, but it showered her in soil crap.

Some women would have chucked something, screamed and fought back.

Sarah Jane just stared at me stupefied, and then began to clean up the pieces, muttering apologies. I'd forgotten how much of a daddy's girl she was, how used to doing what pleased the old man. I was her old man now.

So I made he chuck the whole lot in the dock.

To show I wasn't being too nasty I let her keep one spider plant as long as she kept it on the windowsill in the bog.

We married; a big flash affair with a country church and a marquee in the grounds of Troughton Hall. Honeymoon in The Maldives. Came home to a seat on the board.

It's strange the choices we make in life. Cowards believe in fate, that we have no control over our lives, that we're always working for the Man.

I believe I am the Man because I decided to take control of my life.

It's not easy, as you need to be hard and to know exactly what you want.

I knew what I wanted and I set about planning it as soon as we got back from the honeymoon.

I played the dutiful husband and made sure I kept her well.

Sure, old Troughton made sure she had money of her own, but I made sure she never worked, and I made sure her friends were safe, unthreatening.

I never really let her go to the country.

Her only real taste of the old days was that spider plant on the bathroom window. It was the only plant but I could never forget about it – especially when I was taking a leak. There wasn't much light from the bathroom window, so the thing should have been all brown and scrawny.

It thrived. Damn thing seemed to glow green, them long flat leaves coiled around the pot, slithering over the window ledge, little baby spider plants erupting over it. Spreading.

She really cared for it; watering and pruning.

Even caught her talking to the sodding thing once.

I'd had enough after a while. Told her to cut the frigging thing back before I poured Domestos over it. Looked at me like I'd shagged her mother.

Told her to get out more, see some of her friends up west. She never did.

I'd been thinking how to kill her for a while.

Talked it over with Cheryl.

"Lower. Lower. Yes! Keep pressing. You're getting better, babe."

"Must be all the practice I'm getting."

"And the opportunities, darling. So this mugging ...?"

"I'm paying this acne-ridden housing estate leech to do me over and nick the house keys. God, that's nice, babe!"

"And the dirty deed?"

"Never trust another man to do a job you want to do right. Before I catch the Boston flight. Cab takes me to Heathrow, two hours before. Jag's already been left on Short Stay. Drive back home, into a tracksuit, do the deed, lose the tracksuit, drive back to Heathrow, park up with just enough time to catch the flight."

"Perfect, darling."

"The plan, or what I'm doing?"

"Both."

Told you, I believe I am the Man.

Got myself mugged, got a few bruises, gave a detailed description to the Old Bill. Sarah Jane was in tears when she saw me.

I killed her exactly as planned, two days later, the night before I flew to Boston.

I was flying out with a team, by the way. I was going over in my mind our negotiation strategy while I broke in at home, smashed the place up, and battered her to death. She struggled quite a bit, I'll grant you – kicked me in the balls, but I got her enough times with a spanner to quieten her down.

She tried to get away, made it as far as the bathroom.

Made a right mess. Who'd've thought she had so much blood in her?

Covered the bathroom, even the sodding spider plant.

I dumped the tracksuit and balaclava and went back to Heathrow. Made it back to check-in with only minutes to spare.

Bloody M25. Traffic crawls round it, I can tell you.

The Old Bill met me at the airport when I got back.

Looked like they'd been carved out of something hard and nasty, but they were polite, respectful and full of condolences.

Told me what happened; how the cleaner found her the next day, all the terrible details. How they found the safe broken into, credit cards and jewellery stolen. Suspects. Evidence. Blah, blah, blah.

They interviewed me, of course.

Checked my whereabouts. Did some digging. Interviewed Cheryl, who'd been in all night with her fiancé. Found nothing. Tragic unsolved crime.

Dreadful, the evil in our society. People not safe in their own houses.

I'll admit; the funeral was painful.

I mean, putting up with the Troughtons and the Horse & Hounds set trying to keep their non-existent chins up while we planted her in the family vault took some effort, I can tell you.

The tears were for real!

This is where it gets weird

Because I know what I'm going to tell you is crazy, that proves I'm not mad.

Or stupid. Me and Cheryl left it for over a year before we started seeing each other, and six months after that before she moved in with me.

She was like me, Cheryl.

We had the same tastes; that's why she moved into my place. Loved the way I'd had the place done out (of course, I'd had to redecorate after the murder), all white and clean lines. But she'd only been in a week when she started complaining about the smell.

What smell? I said.

There, she said.

The bathroom? I said.

Yeah, I said.

I went in the bathroom, just to humour her – you know how women get.

I'd really gone to town doing it up. Ice-blue paintwork, white marble bathroom suite, concealed lighting, chrome fittings; and a smell like an old compost heap. The silly cow was right, there was a thick, sweet stench.

The drains backing up, I thought. Something else, too.

It was damp – not wet, but clammy, close, like a sauna or the inside of an old greenhouse. Christ knows where it came from, or the mould between the tiles.

I sacked the cleaner, after I made her clean up the mess and disinfect it.

The old dear was in a right old state, swore blind she cleaned regularly

Senile old cow.

Anyway, the smell came back the next day.

This time it was so strong it made Cheryl puke.

I had to clean it up. Me!

I was finishing up when I noticed something on the windowsill.

Something green, tiny, sprouting between the tiles. I leaned over and stared.

It looked like a tiny speck of grass.

I picked it out and scrubbed the windowsill with bleach, rubbed so hard I ruined the loo brush.

The rotten vegetable smell didn't go away this time, but I got the new cleaner to spray enough disinfectant to keep the compost stink at bay.

But it was still there, underneath.

We were coping with it, though, until Cheryl's dresses.

She spent a fortune on clothes. Unless it was a Name or couture, she wouldn't wear it. You could've fed half of Africa for the price of her collection.

You couldn't've bought a box of matches with what was hanging now in the wardrobes – and a match was what she felt like putting to them when I found her. Not that they'd've burned, splattered with damp and mould, rotten and stinking like they'd been buried in the ground for a year. All of them.

I held her while she cried and raged, and it was then, staring over her shoulder I saw the little weeds, tiny things, sprouting all over the dress.

I reached over and picked one off. It came off as if it had just fallen on the dress. It was tiny, but not as small as the one on the bathroom window.

Bathroom window.

Thin leaves, variegated like a …

I dropped it.

I let go of Cheryl.

I grabbed the dresses, every last rotting stinking one. Tore them from the hangers, tore, tore. I was heaving, swearing as I tore at them, at the dresses.

Cheryl told me afterwards how I pushed her across the room, how the dresses were disintegrating as I grabbed them, how I fell over the step out onto the balcony and twisted my ankle and didn't even notice as I flung the pieces, flung them like filthy snow out over East India Dock; how people gawped up at the loony doing this.

But I'm not mad.

I remember sitting on the bed, silk sheets splattered with filth, and Cheryl screaming at me, screaming, screaming and I'm sitting thinking I'm not here and I'm watching myself staring at my filthy hands while some bitch I'm screwing, a bitch I murdered for sobs and pleads and I don't care.

I feel at peace.

I'm studying a tiny green plant on the floor, one of the dozens scattered all over the bedroom.

Green. Long, thin leaves, variegated with threads that should've been white.

Red.

Tiny spider plants with red stripes. Like veins.

Cheryl must've left the next day.

It wasn't just the stink in the bathroom, the dresses, the damp.

The spiders came back.

They were sprouting from cracks in the balcony paving; they'd burst through the tiles in the kitchen, between the limed-oak panels of the furniture.

It was the spiders on the walls, sprouting from solid brick walls, walls plastered and painted but now green and red where the fully-grown plants seemed to be crawling down the walls. Crawling towards the floor.

Cheryl must have taken one look and left.

At least that's what I suppose happened.

I suppose I must've awoken around noon, slept straight through Cheryl leaving. The sense of calm from the day before still pervaded; had deepened. Y'know that sort of half-sleep, when you're aware but you're floating in a fuzzy cloud of pink wool, and you're mind's scrolling above, between, below through soap bubbles of memory.

I thought I heard a voice.

Could've been Cheryl's, maybe Sarah Jane's, maybe even Ma's.

Couldn't be Ma's, I remember thinking. Dead, just like Sarah Jane.

Time to get up, the voice/voices are saying, not saying.
Leave me alone, I'm saying back, I got rid of you.
Time to face the world, the voice/voices whisper.

They recede, and I'm suddenly happy, so at peace. And I'm waking and it's so warm, warm, warm, and I open my eyes and I'm looking through a sparkling window. It's so beautiful, so glittering. So glistening. So wet.

I sat up and suddenly I was afraid.

The French doors out onto the balcony were fogged, dripping with condensation. Then I saw the spiders, as Cheryl must have seen them earlier.

Saw them all down the walls around me, and saw their variegated green/red leaves a carpet over the floor.

I suppose I screamed.

It's difficult to remember, but I know I jumped onto the bedside table, grabbed my dressing gown, chucked it onto the awful floor, and used it to step on and stumble and flounder out of the bedroom onto the polished parquet of the lounge area. My hands and arms ached for some reason.

I took in the ceiling, walls covered in spider plants, fronds almost brushing the floor, but not there yet.

It's a big lounge area, the part of the apartment that most resembles the warehouse it used to be. I glanced behind.

They'd followed me out of the bedroom, spreading out across the parquet towards me.

But I never saw them move.

They were just there, closer, like that game where you close your eyes, and they creep up on you and if you don't hear them they've got you.

But in that game they made noises.

It's a big room.

I couldn't keep my eye on everywhere at once, and I had to cross the room, and every step I took, every move of my head I saw them closer, closer, closer.

Surrounding me. Cutting me off from the front door.

I suppose the way one of the steel uplights was bent and battered, and with those gouges found in the floor, I must've used it to thrash at the plants.

It'd explain the pain in my arms and hands. Yes, that's it; I attacked the plants with the uplighter, thrashing my way through into the hallway.

And the bloodstains were mine.

I couldn't have seen a giant, obscene spider plant, erupting out of the hall floor, variegated leaves as thick as your thigh. Variegated green and red, like veins. Pulsing.

I'm sure all those bloodstains didn't happen when I raised the uplighter and tore into the plant – slashed, thrashed; gouts of blood erupting, splattering from the veins.

I had to attack it, see.

One of those obscene fronds held Cheryl, was wrapped around her neck.

Her eyes pleaded with me, her tongue stuck out, like a fat red leaf.

I stared past her to the bathroom door, open.

Slick with blood and sweat, I must have retreated to the bathroom.

It was the toilet bowl.

I definitely struck it as I fell, as I looked up at the spider plant, the one I'd thrown away, now back on the windowsill.

It was when I reached up to grab the thing that something stopped me.

Something grabbed my arm; something began to pull me back out of the bathroom.

Yes, I know that.

Yes, I know how the cleaner found me, found Cheryl in the hall.

How I was naked and curled up in a ball by the toilet.

Yes, I was babbling I suppose, about Sarah Jane, about Ma, about Cheryl.

Look, I accept there were no spider plants found anywhere; except the one off the windowsill the cleaner found me eating.

The one I'd thrown away last year.
They spread, though, spiders.

edited by Stephanie Ellis & S.G. Mulholland

Olé Bubba and the Forty Steves
by James S. Dorr

"Ollie! Ollie!" the crowds were shouting, that lined the narrow, cobblestoned street, shops and houses pressing its sides so close it was like running through some kind of tunnel. "Ollie! Ollie!" like they must of thought maybe that was my name -- like there I was, a real "Ollie Bubba!" -- 'cept Miss Margie Ann told me after it's just some kind of thing Spanish folk say, and they don't even spell it right.

Like how they spell it is 'o-l-é' with a funny diddle mark over the 'e'.

But Margie Ann's real smart, having got a whole year of college down at Tulane, before she came to Pamplona to work in this rundown taberna -- that's how they say 'bar' here -- on some kind of summer exchange student thing. And she's good folk too, being from Baton Rouge. Cajun stock, she told me. Which didn't help me one little bit, running as I was, forty angry men all named 'Steve' chasing me, tourists like me from the U. S. of A. 'cepting these forty Steve's was fixing to eat me should I slow down and let them catch me, a half dozen Spanish bulls chasing after them, snorting and threatening to stick us all with their horns. And what was worse I was starting to get nervous.

I tried to think, which folks back home tell me is not my strongest point, but which gives me pause and tends to calm me down. How had it happened, me getting myself in this mess in the first place, like some kind of weird Arabian Nights dream? How had it all started?

My thoughts went back to just two days before ...

***

... or rather it was already night by then, when I stood outside the Sesame Hotel, its blinking neon sign proclaiming:
'OPEN'

Or more to the point the hotel bar was open too, with its own sign underneath another, bigger one: 'Welcome American "Steves" Convention' -- Margie Ann told me after it was like some kind of reunion, it had been in the paper and all, of guys from the U. S. of A. all named 'Steve' -- but, to the point again, these were in English. I mean good, proper American English, not even that hoity-toity England stuff that they use on the signs in train stations.

And inside I heard voices talking in English too.

So I went in myself. I could see right away that it wasn't really my kind of place, fellas at the tables all wearing suits and ties. Yankees. Yuppies. Not even students who sometimes look scruffy but half the time underneath are really good, plain folk -- you know the kind I mean. But anyhow, here, I just sat up at the bar, which was okay with me.

Shoot, the thing was I was only trying to find some place where I could tell the bartender, "Beer," and what I'd get would be just a glass of beer. Not some kind of quiz. Not some 'twenty questions' game: "Cerveza, Senor? Parda? Clara?"

How do you just say Blue Ribbon in Spanish?

Shucks, I don't have a clue, foreign tongues like that not being my thing. You know what I mean.

But here they had a good, cold, rich draft beer which, in fact, went down so good that I had another. And maybe another. And one after that, too -- shoot, I don't know how many. All I know is that, after a few more, I had to go pee.

I mean really pee -- you know how beer is, how it sometimes sneaks up on you. So I told the barkeep, "Save my stool, please," and went off a looking to find the john.

You'll never guess the one set of signs it didn't occur to them to put in English!

And my bladder was telling me, ain't no time to find someone to ask. You got to go quick.

So I picked me a sign, one that said 'Mujeres,' which I figured maybe was Spanish for 'Mules'. Which I figured was close enough, under the circumstance.

By the time I was inside, I'd already unzipped, and then I noticed there wasn't no urinals. But then that's foreign toilets for you, they do strange things, so I just beelined my way to a stall.

It had a seat and all so I just figured -- hey, what the heck, I'd just ease my pants down and get myself comfy. Maybe save me a trip later that way.

But then I heard a commotion as more people came into that rest room, just outside my stall -- women's voices a jabbering in English, but Yankee-type English. Like these were the Steve's wives.

So I just sat where I was, real quiet, and peeped out a little through the crack where the door shuts – so's to know when they'd left, you understand, so I could make my getaway too. Except I was also beginning to get nervous.

Now I got to tell you when I get nervous, it goes down and starts twisting around in my bowels. Get me nervous enough, I break wind -- I mean sometimes I nearly shit out through my pants. Now my pants being down at the moment, me on the john and all, that was okay, but when I say I break wind, I mean I really fart.

Like ring-tailed snorters got nothing on me, but the thing was I couldn't let them hear me, 'cause then they'd know I was there. While meanwhile they was jabbering and all that and -- which didn't help my nervousness any -- some of them now were starting to take out knives. Knives with blood on them. And some of them, I could see through the crack, were gnawing on something, passing it around, you know, and it looked like a human arm!

So there I was, staying still, trying my best to hold my cheeks together, to maybe let it out slow and silent -- feeling the gas building -- hoping that maybe if they caught the smell, they'd think it was one of theirs. When all of a sudden another one of these Steve's wives came in.

This one had another girl with her, a little senorita I'd already had my eye on in the bar, 'cept she wasn't one of them. She was kicking and carrying on like, until this new Steve's wife pulled her own knife out, saying, "I brought us the main course."

And the senorita SCREAMED!

That was enough for me! I let go too, then. Roaring and blasting, like earthquakes full of farts -- I swear I nearly rose up from that throne on a cloud of brown rocket-gas -- and I was out that stall. One hand holding my pants halfway up, grabbing that little senorita up in my other arm, Steve's wives gagging and retching around us -- that smell was something, too, holding it in so long -- and half of them knocked to the floor from the blast alone.

Me still pooting and bubbling like earthquake aftershocks -- helping to keep those Steve's wives back. Out through the bathroom door, out through the barroom, out to the street beyond --

When a voice went: "Psst!"

I half stopped. "Huh?"

"Psst. In here, stupid." The voice was in English. A lady's voice in good down home American.

I felt her hand take mine, still looking back as I felt her lead me, waiting, you see, for those Steves's wives to come pouring out the Sesame Hotel door, blood in their eyes, a coming after me for taking away their dinner.

But then we were safe, in a basement of some sort, the senorita crying silently in a corner. My rescuer facing me.

"Sorry, you know, for what I called you. Outside on the street, but we did have to hurry." She held out her hand to shake. "My name's Margie Ann."

"Margie Ann?" I said. "Real pleased to meet you. Most of the folks back home just call me Bubba."

***

That's how we spent the night, comparing notes, except Margie Ann had to go back upstairs till it was real late, because upstairs was this Spanish bar where she worked as a sort of assistant manager.

Which meant she ran the place, since the owner was mostly drunk.

She set me later to cleaning glasses, and told the senorita in Spanish -- I think I already said Margie Ann was smart -- to help wait tables. And Margie Ann explained to me about how she'd read in the Spanish papers that this disease or something had struck in the United States -- must have been just after I'd left, having won this trip to Pamplona in a contest down at the Farm Bureau that had to do with places where they raised bulls -- but anyhow it only made Yuppies sick. Not good old boys and their womenfolk like us, had something to do with us eating barbecue which, Margie Ann said, they had in Spain too if you knew where to look.

Like some kind of antidote to the disease -- she showed me a rack of hot barbecue sauce she'd bought for the bar here, 'cause sometimes she helped with the cooking too. But back to the point, when the Yuppies got sick, most everyone died -- in fact, according to Margie Ann's paper, it was even killing folks here in Spain, though mostly in big cities that got more tourists -- and those that pulled through came out of it with an insatiable desire to chow down on humans.

"You mean like those Steve's wives I saw in that ladies room?" I asked.

"Uh huh," she said. "Though most of them don't seem to like the Spanish. I mean for eating -- something about their flesh being too spicy -- that's why they seem mostly to still look for folks like us. And what were you doing in a ladies room anyway?"

"Well, uh," I stammered. "Uh, I think I just heard something outside?"

I really just meant to change the subject. By then it was real late, the bar already closed, the senorita asleep on a cot, and just me and Margie Ann still up and talking. Me still cleaning glasses -- it had been a busy night. All of the regular, good old Spanish boys, excepting, of course, none of them spoke English. In fact, it was almost dawn.

"I'll look," she said. She opened the front door and -- I dropped the beer mug I'd just finished polishing!

On the door was a sign, chalk-marked and in English: 'THIS WAY TO THE BUBBA'.

"Y-you think maybe one of them Steve's wives wrote that?" I asked. "Maybe one of them sneaked after us, real quiet, and found where you took me, then wrote that there so she wouldn't forget, so tonight they'll be able to find me and get me?"

Margie Ann wiped it off. "Maybe," she answered. "Either that or the fact we're directly across the street from the hotel where they seem to be staying. Meanwhile, though ..."

She bent down and picked up the mug I'd dropped, and I saw that I'd busted the handle clean off. "Gee, I'm sorry," I started, but she just reached up on a shelf and brought down a tube marked in English: 'Superior Glue'.

"Something else I picked up when I bought that American barbecue sauce," she said. "The boss here is cheap. We're always breaking glasses like that, but he never gets new ones."

With just two drops she had that handle back on good as new and twice as strong. Then after she'd cooked us a little breakfast, she showed me a place in the back room to sleep. "Big evening tonight," she said. "Tomorrow's the start of the Fiesta de San Fermin -- sort of a patron saint around here -- when they run the bulls, so get your rest, 'cause it's going to be plenty busy later on."

***

I must have been dreaming about my lucky escape that last night, and about how Margie Ann had saved me, because I could hear her voice in my sleep. "Psst!"

Right in my ear: "Psst!"

I yawned and rolled over -- then felt something shaking me!

"Psst. Bubba, wake up. There's something funny. A delivery truck came into the alley a half hour ago, and unloaded forty big crates marked 'Glassware.' I had to sign for them and had them take them down into the cellar ..."

"So?" I said. "You told me they're always breaking beer glasses, and that tonight's the night before that Fiesta de Santa Fe something so you're expecting lots of customers. Stands to reason they'd lay in a new supply ..."

"Three things, Bubba," she said. "First, I'm the one who usually does the ordering, not the boss -- he just tells me what to get. Second, I told you before the boss is a cheapskate, that it took me most of a whole day even to get him to let me buy glue to repair the ones that are broken already. And third, those labels are in English, not Spanish."

"So?" I said.

So she made me get dressed and follow her downstairs into the cellar, the senorita following behind us holding a flashlight. She tapped the first box, and a voice whispered back: "Is it time yet to get him?"

A woman's voice, just like the ones in the ladies room!

"Uh, not yet," she answered. She made her voice deep, with a Yuppie accent. "Get some sleep first, then I'll let you know when it's time."

"Okay," the voice answered.

Then Margie Ann tapped the second box and it answered back too, and the third and the fourth and I don't know how many -- Margie Ann answering each one just the way she had before -- except Margie Ann told me after she'd counted them up again to make sure it was exactly forty. But now we snuck back upstairs and Margie Ann reached and got down that tube of Superior Glue and some labels and marking pens and such, then got on the phone. Then she went back down with the senorita to hold the light, this time having me wait upstairs for her.

About ten minutes later she came back upstairs just in time for a big delivery truck to back into the alley. "I told them there'd been a mistake," she told me. "I told them the crates were supposed to be shipped to Abu Dhabi, C.O.D. of course. That's after I put the new labels on them."

She held up the now almost empty tube of Superior Glue. "That's after I glued them shut."

"Uh, isn't Abu Dhabi someplace near Iraq?" I asked.

She shrugged. "It was the first place I thought of. Anyway it ought to keep the Steve's wives busy -- and out of your hair."

She sort of snuggled up to me then and ran a hand through that aforementioned hair. Me doing my best not to melt into a puddle.

"Of course," she continued, "there is one more worry ..."

***

... The Steve's themselves! Forty -- count 'em, forty. One for each Steve's wife, now safely shipped off to Abu Dhabi.

But along around midnight, some of those Steve's must have missed their wives. In ones and twos they started to drift in -- you could tell them by how they dressed, in suits and ties, and the fact they only spoke in English.

Yankee English.

I hid behind the bar, keeping real low while I cleaned the glasses, while the senorita disguised herself as some kind of veiled, oriental dancing girl, just in case she'd been seen the night before in the Sesame Hotel. Margie Ann, herself, would be safe since they didn't know who she was, but she kept giving the Steve's free refills -- not too many, of course, but enough to get them to buy her drinks too and let her into their conversations.

So the night went on, busy as she had said -- more Steve's drifting in, in threes and fours now -- so busy in fact that the bar didn't close at all. Even when morning came people were still drinking.

That's when Margie Ann went back behind the bar, pressing a paper into my hand.

"It's a street map," she said. "The Steve's are going to make their move as soon as the sun is up. Let them chase you, but follow this map. It'll take you to the city's Old Quarter. I'll follow after, too, but then I'll take a short cut to get ahead as soon as you get there. Then listen for me to shout directions."

"Uh, you say I'm supposed to let the Steve's chase me?"

"Uh huh," she said. "Then when you get to where the map takes you, listen for my directions."

"Uh, they're gonna chase me?"

She nodded. "Yes. Look, Bubba, I have an idea -- it's the only thing I can think of to save you. But do as I say, okay?"

Somehow it didn't seem okay to me, that chasing part, I mean. That is, I used to be a good enough runner in high school, when I was back on the football team, but that was a couple of racks of ribs and kegs of beer in the past, if you catch what I mean. While these cannibal Yuppie Steve guys looked like they actually did exercise --

"Bubba," Margie Ann whispered, "it's almost time. Remember, when you're out the door turn right."

"Look, Margie Ann, I'm kind of getting nervous."

"I know," she whispered. "Look, try to hold it in until it seems like things can't get any worse, okay?"

Then she kissed me.

Which brings me to here, all the crowds shouting "Ollie! Ollie!" Me ahead of the whole pack. It had been almost like floating on air, I mean after that kiss. It was like I was drifting, following the twists and turns on the map, heading into the city's old section with shouts and screams of the Yuppies behind me. Gnashings of teeth. But somehow, by miracle, me just ahead of them.

Then seeing Margie Ann again -- just a glimpse -- shouting, "Turn left, Bubba!" Then another block – "Turn right!"

That's when I found myself on this narrow street, forty Yuppies pounding the cobblestoned pavement behind me. Shouting: "Slow down! A healthy day has to start with a good breakfast!"

With me the breakfast.

And someone else shouting, "Los Toros! Los Toros!" And all of a sudden me realizing I knew one word in Spanish.

Hooves thundering! Horns flashing! Knives and forks clashing as hunger-crazed Yuppie zombies drew forth their tableware --

Me starting to get nervous?

Boy, I got nervous! I let out a blast like a trumpet fanfare -- the crowds shouting louder, "Ollie! Ollie! Ollie! Ollie!" Me blaring the sound of a whole danged brass band, tubas and flugelhorns and cornets and all. French horns and trombones.

And that was just openers.

Because I got nervous all over the place, spewing brown plumes behind me. Thunder and cymbal crash! Buildings shook! Women screamed!

Small children fainted!

Crescendos on crescendos, scales and arpeggios. Volcanic eruptions!

And me, I was just warming up to nervous --

When all of a sudden I heard Margie Ann's voice: "Bubba, it's okay."

"Huh?" I said, as she ran out to greet me. The crowds throwing flowers.

"Ollie! Ollie!"

Behind me I saw where the Yuppies had fallen, victims of that first blast. Maybe not fallen, but slowed enough that the bulls caught up with them, goring and tossing and trampling them underfoot. All of that action slowing the bulls down too.

Then the smell got to them -- I was told afterwards, after they'd made mincemeat out of the forty Steves, all six bulls just stopped and fainted and died. Right there on the spot.

And Margie Ann kissed me, just right out in front of everyone like that, and people were shouting, and throwing more roses. 'Course some said that that was to help cover up the smell. Saying the running of the bulls at Pamplona would never be the same -- not since the day Ollie Bubba had showed them how.

Afterwards I was awarded the ears and tails of the bulls -- another custom the Spanish folk have, according to Margie Ann. They took them to us on a kind of pillow thing, right to the taberna where Margie Ann worked and where I was now staying. I didn't know what to do with them myself.

But Margie Ann smiled. "Just hand me some of that sauce first," she said, leading me to the kitchen. She got out a big pot. "Then we're going to have us some Cajun style cooking."

edited by Stephanie Ellis & S.G. Mulholland

The Dreams that Stuff is Made Of
by William Meikle

"Make it realistic," they said. "This is 1953, not 1933."

What they expected him to do with a three thousand dollar budget was a mystery to Doug Turner. Originally he had planned to do it in stop-motion, but the bean counters were having none of that.

"Harryhausen is finished," they said. "Audiences want more realism. And make it big. People like big."

After a bit of head scratching he took them at their word. He even took the quest for realism a bit too literally. Buying twenty gorilla pelts on the black market cost nearly half his budget, and some sleepless nights wondering whether the authorities would find out about the museum in Rhodesia that had been pilfered to fulfil his order when they came up short on live catches. Then he had to get the wardrobe people to work overtime to stitch it all together. He had to call in every favour in his book for that one.

By the time he'd organised a midnight raid into the country to steal enough straw to stuff the sewn skins he was starting to feel more like a criminal than a FX specialist. And after three more days trying to get the head -- and the mouth in particular, right, he was starting to feel he should be anything other than a FX specialist.

But when, right on schedule, the bean counters turned up to view the star of their new movie, Doug was sure they'd be impressed with the twenty-foot monster that stood on the soundstage.

He didn't get the expected reaction.

They laughed.

Then they berated him, long and hard, for wasting their money. Doug was told in no uncertain terms that his future in the business depended on him getting it sorted. Quite how that was to be done was never mentioned, but they were most insistent on the matter.

Doug took to the bottle for the weekend.

***

Once he got sober the situation looked no better. He was on the verge of walking away from the job completely when he had a visitor.

At first Doug was lost in his own reverie, staring at the sad sack of straw and hair that stood in the otherwise empty soundstage and wondering just how he'd ever convinced himself that it would work. It looked less like a monster than he'd hoped, more like an oversized stuffed toy. The eyes looked exactly like what they were; globes of plastic stuck on with glue, one slightly askew giving the giant ape a comical squint. One of the false teeth he'd had mocked up out of papier-mâché had already fallen out leaving a gap on the left hand side, and the bottom jaw hung open just too far, making the beast look more imbecilic than frightening.

He was on the verge of setting fire to it when a hand touched his shoulder. There was a small man at his side. His skin looked like old polished leather that had been left to age, and he looked so thin as to be almost skeletal. But his blue eyes danced with life and his laughter echoed loudly around the soundstage when he looked at the ape.

"So this is why my prize exhibit was stolen? I must say, it looks better here than in a museum."

Doug was at a loss how to reply.

"I guess there's no use denying it," he finally said resignedly. "How much do I owe you?"

The little man laughed again. It was so infectious that Doug couldn't help but join him.

"Nothing," the little man said. "As I said, it looks better here. But it would look even better in motion."

Now it was Doug's turn to laugh.

"That would be a good trick. Sadly it is only a dream."

The little man put a hand on Doug's shoulder again.

"Then a dream it shall be. But you must dream through African eyes."

Doug blinked.

***

He was surrounded by greenery, and rain pattered down to drum on leaves the size of dinner plates. He swung, fluid and effortless, through branches of tall trees, roaring his joy at life, at freedom.

***

Doug blinked again.

The stuffed ape had moved. It now no longer stood upright. It was bent over, knuckles balancing it in a pose that looked almost belligerent. The squint was gone. Even the gap in the teeth looked more natural. The fur seemed to bristle, as if ruffled by wind.

"What just happened?" Doug said.

The little man laughed again.

"You dreamed the African dream. The gorilla pelt from the museum wasn't just a pelt. It was once a man, a great sorcerer and shape-changer. The pelt remembers. The pelt dreams – of past glories, and freedom."

Doug laughed.

"That's the best pitch I've heard in years. Seriously... what kind of whammy did you put on me?"

The little man showed Doug a smile. There was a gap in the top row that made the grin look lopsided.

"There is no whammy – just faith. Gorillas are made to be free by their God, as are we. And their God has leant us some of his own flesh for this enterprise. Watch and learn."

The man started to hum; a deep bass vibration that rattled Doug's teeth. He lifted an arm.

The ape responded.

A huge hairy arm raised high above the ape's head. The little man started to walk forward. The ape rose from the sitting position and walked across the soundstage. This was not a thing of skin and straw. Muscles bunched beneath the skin and although the pelts seemed to hang slackly off an emaciated body, there was more than enough animal power on display to send Doug shuttling backwards quickly, looking for the exit.

The ape stopped at exactly the same time as the small man who stood beneath its swollen belly, dwarfed by the upright creature. The man seemed unconcerned. He opened his arms wide then slapped at his chest with his palms, a quick drum-roll. The ape followed suit, at the same time bellowing a roar of defiance across the soundstage.

Doug stopped being frightened. He was looking at the ape, but in his mind's eye he was seeing the movie, the beast rising up out of thick jungle to terrorise a terrified group of intrepid explorers.

This just might work.

He stood and moved to the small man's side, trying to ignore the creature above them.

"Can you do that to order?" Doug said.

The little man smiled, showing the gap in his teeth.

So did the ape.

***

It took Doug a couple of days to set it up. He had to take out an overdraft to pay for the foliage he wanted, and even used up all the money in his wallet to get some extras onto the soundstage and primed.

During the whole two days the stuffed ape sat in the corner of the soundstage, head bowed as if asleep. At times Doug wondered whether he'd dreamed the whole earlier experience, or whether he was finally succumbing to the delirium tremens his alcohol consumption surely merited. The small man, who eventually introduced himself as Mr. Mkele, put paid to that idea. All it took was for him to place a hand on Doug's shoulder, and he was back in the jungle again.

Running free.

As the deadline to the screen test grew closer, Doug's anxiety levels grew in proportion, but the little African man was never far away, and always willing to allow Doug access to the dream. It became the once place where he could feel no pressure, no worry, just the joy of rain in his face and a freedom of action unconstrained by money and bean counters. The dream sustained him through to the Friday morning on the soundstage, and the arrival of those bean counters to see the ape.

When Doug saw the mass of foliage arrayed across the set, and the extras dressed in pith helmets and khaki, he actually smiled and started to relax.

There's no way this is going to fail.

The screen test itself went like clockwork. The drummer, who Doug persuaded to work for a pack of cigarettes and a fifth of rye, set up a rock-solid beat as the explorers entered the jungle. Mr. Mkele added some verisimilitude by raising his voice in a singsong chant that seemed to vibrate through the whole stage and set the foliage rustling as if in wind. Right on cue the ape rose up out of the greenery, slapped its palms against its chest and bellowed.

An extra fainted, the bean counters applauded, and everyone said all the right things.

Two hours later they axed the movie, killing the project stone dead.

"We want to do something with tentacles, something in stop motion. Harrryhausen is hot this year."

***

Doug went home and made a start on drinking himself to oblivion.

"Those men are wrong," Mr. Mkele said. He sat across the table, not drinking, but not stopping Doug from doing so. "Your city needs to see what the jungle is like. Your city needs to see freedom. You need to see freedom."

Doug took a swig direct from a bottle of rye; his third, or maybe it was his fourth – he was already starting to lose count.

"Freedom seems a heck of a long way away my friend," he said.

"That is because you have forgotten the dream."

Doug slugged down more rye.

"Not forgotten," he said. "But what good does it do me now?"

Things started to get foggy, but he heard the little man's words well enough.

"You just have to have faith in the dream. There is still time to show them the power of the free."

***

Doug opened his eyes to a wash of fuzzy green that only slowly came into focus. He was lying in thick foliage. As his eye focussed he realised he was back on the soundstage, in the artificial jungle.

I really tied one on this time.

He stood, shaky on unsteady legs.

A janitor was sweeping the set, an older man that Doug barely knew. He had his back turned, lost in his brushing.

"Hi," Doug said. It came out as a deep rumble. He cleared his throat. The old janitor turned, looked up and fled, screaming. It was only then that Doug started to suspect something wasn't quite right.

He seemed to be too big, too bulky. He raised a hand towards his face, and screamed at the sight of a broad hand, covered in this coarse hair, with broken dirty nails. That wasn't the worst part – the hand was nearly three feet across. He screamed again. It came out as a bellow that echoed around the soundstage. A security cop arrived at the door and immediately raised a pistol and fired. Doug saw the flash, but felt no impact.

He missed.

But he was wrong in that. He looked down to see a hole in his side, pieces of dry straw poking out of it.

"Hey," he shouted.

The whole set vibrated, and the security guard dropped his gun. He too fled.

Doug lumbered towards the door. He was too big to fit through. He put up a hand to push the tall sliding door aside. It fell away into the road outside with a crash.

Somewhere people started to scream but Doug scarcely noticed. Something was very wrong. He seemed to be inside the ape.

Living the dream.

A nee-naw wail heralded the approach of several police squad cars that screeched to a halt out in the lot beyond the soundstage. More shots rang out and puffs of straw flew. Doug yelled again.

"Hey, stop shooting at me!"

It came out as a roar that shook the whole street, and several of the police officers backed away fast. Doug took his chance and broke into a run but, uncoordinated as he was, and unused to the sheer bulk of this body he stumbled into one of the patrol cars. He swatted it with a hand and the car flew ten yards in the air before landing with a crump of glass and metal. The shooting got more intensive.

Doug fled in the opposite direction from the gunfire – and straight onto the exterior set where they were filming a western. He stumbled, almost fell, and demolished the whole façade of a street, the thin wood splintering beneath him. Horses whinnied, women screamed, and more police cars arrived.

This isn't going to end well.

Doug had no plan beyond escaping the shooting policemen. He bounded through the western set, scattering film crew and extras to all corners, before he realised that continuing in that direction would take him to the heart of the city.

He stopped running, but that allowed the police to blow more holes in his body. Straw flew everywhere. He was seriously considering just standing still, letting them take him down, when he heard a singsong chant that he recognised. It seemed to come from the hills to the east of the city. Doug turned in that direction and broke into a run. More shots followed behind him but none hit him, at least none that he felt. Sirens wailed, and screams rang out—sounds he almost recognised—sounds of the jungle. He felt free as he bounded through suburban streets past the shocked faces of homeowners and children, knocking cars and trees aside if they got in his way. All he could think of now was the song.

It led him high to the hill overlooking the city, to the large letters of the HOLLYWOOD sign. There was a car parked beside the sign, and a small man stood beside the open driver's door. He was the source of the song. As Doug slowed from his headlong rush he saw another person, slumped in the passenger seat.

That's me!

Mr. Mkele's song rose to a crescendo.

Doug blinked.

***

And woke up sitting in the car, staring out at the HOLLYWOOD sign, and a giant ape trying to tear it apart.

"Quick," Mr. Mkele shouted. "The sorcerer has been awakened. We do not have much time."

Doug pushed himself groggily out of the car. The little man was already running, not away from the ape, but towards it. He was carrying a bulky kerosene container. There was another on the ground beside the car, and Doug immediately saw the intent.

He means to burn it.

Mr. Mkele had reached the sign and had already started sloshing kerosene around as Doug lugged the other can over towards him. The ape paid them no attention, seeming intent on tearing the HOLLYWOOD sign apart. Even as Doug arrived beside the smaller man and joined him in pouring the kerosene the ape managed to tear the leftmost O from its moorings and threw it, like a discus, down towards the city where it swooped away out of view. The beast roared its defiance and slapped at its chest, but now that he was closer Doug could see that it was already badly damaged. Several large rents ran down its left side, straw having already fallen in a pile at the ape's feet. Enough had escaped to make the body look strangely deflated.

And that was not all. One of the stitched seams in the head had split and more straw was already falling from it. The beast was not finished yet though. Even as Mr. Mkele flipped a lighter and tossed it at the creature's feet it had torn the H from the sign and was using it to beat the rest of the sign to a broken pile of wood and plastic.

The flame took it fast. With one last statement of defiance the ape stood tall, slapped its chest, and roared, long and loud before falling in on itself in a shower of flaming straw that danced away in the wind.

***

Later, on their way back down the hill, and while the Army and police were headed up in the other direction, Doug finally decided to ask the question that had been bothering him.

"What just happened?"

He got an answer, but maybe not the one he was expecting.

"The city has seen," Mr. Mkele said. "And you have shown your skill. I believe your bean counters will now be more than keen to procure your services. And I shall be more than willing to help you. For you see the sorcerer could take more forms than just the ape."

The little man laughed, showing the gap in his teeth. "Would you like a crocodile skin stripped from the still living body of an ancient god?"

edited by Stephanie Ellis & S.G. Mulholland

ABOUT THE CONTRIBUTORS

After thirty years at sea, **Ross Baxter** now concentrates on writing sci-fi and horror fiction. His varied work has been published in print and Kindle by a number of publishing houses in both the US and the UK. Married to a Norwegian and with two Anglo-Viking kids, he now lives in Derby, England.
amazon.com/author/rossbaxter
rossbaxter.wordpress.com

James Brogden is a part-time Australian who grew up in Tasmania and now lives with his wife and two daughters in Bromsgrove, Worcestershire, where he teaches English. His short fiction has appeared in various places ranging from *The Big Issue* to the BFS Award-winning Alchemy Press, who will be releasing a collection of his short stories in July 2015. His novels, published by Snowbooks, include the Birmingham-based urban fantasy *The Narrows* and the steampunk/horror *Tourmaline* – the sequel to which was released in May 2015. Blogging occurs at **jamesbrogden.blogspot.co.uk** and tweeting at **@skippybe**.

Jon Charles is a teacher, occasional film extra and horror writer based in the West Country of England. His darkly comic stories have also appeared in several issues of *Far Horizons* magazine. A novel is on the way.

edited by Stephanie Ellis & S.G. Mulholland

David Croser was born in Carlisle, Cumbria; a distant land of mountains, valleys and lakes, the land of Wordsworth and the wild borderland between England and Scotland. He went to university in Nottingham and has lived in Cardiff and Bristol before settling in Birmingham, where he now lives. When not writing scary stories, he teaches, reads comics and likes very long car journeys in the most amazing country in the world. His literary heroes are MR James, HP Lovecraft, John Harvey and Terrance Dicks. He is the author of *Rice Pudding Reality*, a collection of his scary stories, available through Amazon and as an ebook; it can also be ordered old skool as a paperback through **createspace.com**. Go on, make his mum proud.

Indiana writer **James Dorr**'s *The Tears of Isis* was a 2013 Bram Stoker Award® nominee for Superior Achievement in a Fiction Collection. Other books include *Strange Mistresses: Tales of Wonder and Romance*, *Darker Loves: Tales of Mystery and Regret* and his all-poetry *Vamps (A Retrospective)*. With nearly 400 appearances from Alfred Hitchcock's *Mystery Magazine* to *Yellow Bat Review*, Dorr invites readers to visit his blog at **jamesdorrwriter.wordpress.com**.

Stephanie Ellis is currently a Teaching Assistant in a Southampton secondary school, but previously worked for many years as a technical author. Her genre fiction short stories have found success with a variety of publishers including Alchemy Press, Death Throes Publishing, Poporn Horror, KnightWatch Press, Mystery and Horror LLC, Visionary Press and Sky Warrior Books as well as *Sanitarium* magazine and *Massacre Magazine*. Her poetry, quite often of a dark nature, has been published in local and national press, *FarOffPlaces Magazine*, *What the Dickens* ezine and their related *The Busker* anthology. Samples of her writing can be found at **stephellis.weebly.com** and she is on Twitter at **@el_stevie**.

Richard Freeman is the Zoological Director of the Centre for Fortean Zoology, the world's only full-time mystery animal research organisation. As a cryptozoologist he has tracked many strange creatures across the world, including the Tasmanian wolf, the almasty, the Mongolian deathworm, the orang-pendek, the giant anaconda and the yeti. He has written widely on cryptozoology but has recently expanded into horror and weird fiction with two collections of short stories: *Green Unpleasant Land: Eighteen stories of British Horror* and *Hyankmonogatari: Tales of Japanese Horror*. **cfz.co.uk**

Scott Harper works in the waste management industry, otherwise known as law enforcement. In between buying every vampire DVD, book, comic or collectible that comes out, he sometimes finds time to write. His stories have appeared in *Best New Vampire Tales* and *Space and Time Magazine*. He lives in California with his wife, son and dog Otis.

Stewart Hotston crossed the road to escape the puns on the other side. Once there he discovered that when the man with the spade on his head left he had the dugout all to himself. Well, except for the vegetarian zombies, but all they wanted was grains. After that he tried to show a friendly vampire how to use his smartphone, but it was a waste of time as the fiend was a bluddite. So he retired to his shed to work on more stories as a way to escape his mundane and practical life. He one bought a couple of parrots to keep him company while he worked but got rid of them when he heard one turn to another on the perch they were sharing and say "Can you smell fish?"

O.L. Humphreys grew up in the Royal Forest of Dean, Gloucestershire, but now lives in the West London suburb of Ealing with his wife Daniele. However he began writing short fiction whilst living in Northampton, where he joined a science fiction writers group. His physical appearance could be described as somewhere between a quantity surveyor and structural engineer, but with a beard. On the whole he has a placid, easygoing temperament; however, he is likely to fly into a rage if his cider is served over ice. To date his only other published short story is *Minefields and Meadows* in *Dark Lane Anthology Volume 1* published by NoodleDoodle Publications.

Lisamarie Lamb started writing in her late teens but it was only with the birth of her daughter that she decided to write more seriously, with the aim of publication. Since that decision in 2010, she has had almost 40 short stories published in anthologies and magazines. She also works as a freelance writer for *insideKENT* magazine. In November 2012, Dark Hall Press published a collection of her short stories with a twist, entitled *Over The Bridge*. In November 2013, J. Ellington Ashton Press released a second short story collection entitled *Fairy Lights*. April 2014 saw the publication of her first children's book, *The Book of Mandragore* (J. Ellington Ashton). She has collaborated on – and edited – a project entitled *A Roof Over Their Heads*, written by six authors from the Isle of Sheppey about the island where she used to live with her husband, daughter and two cats. Since then, she has added a rabbit to the family and moved to Hartley, where she now lives next door to a field full of horses.
themoonlitdoor.blogspot.co.uk
facebook.com/lisamarielambwriter

T.M. "Tim" McLean is an editor as well as an author. His love of fiction led to him starting his own publishing company, NoodleDoode Publications, where he seeks to discover and publish the best stories the independent writing community has to offer. So far Tim's short stories have been published in a number of anthologies, including *Serrated: Tormenting Tales of the Macabre*, *Tales from the Perseus Arm Volume 2*, *Terror at the Beach* and *Fear's Accomplice*. Many more of his short stories are due for publication in 2015. Tim's editing credits include *Zombies Galore* (KnightWatch Press), *Loch Shock* (Silent Fray Productions) and *Fear's Accomplice: Halloween* (NoodleDoode Publications). For more information visit **facebook.com/noodledoodlepub** or follow Tim **@timmclean2**.

Ken MacGregor's work has appeared in dozens of anthologies, magazines and podcasts. In 2013, a collection of his short stories, called *An Aberrant Mind*, was released by Sirens Call Publications. Ken is a member of The Great Lakes Association of Horror Writers and an Affiliate member of HWA. Ken's the kind of guy that, if he found himself stranded somewhere with you, would probably eat you to survive. Ken lives in Michigan with his family and two unstable cats. His author website is **ken-macgregor.com**.

William Meikle is a Scottish writer, now living in Canada, with twenty novels published in the genre press and over 300 short story credits in thirteen countries. He has books available from a variety of publishers including Dark Regions Press, DarkFuse and Dark Renaissance, and his work has appeared in a number of professional anthologies and magazines with recent sales to *Nature Future*, *Penumbra* and *Buzzy Mag* among others. He lives in Newfoundland with whales, bald eagles and icebergs for company. When he's not writing he drinks beer, plays guitar and dreams of fortune and glory.

An Australian-born English writer, **Steve Mulholland** went through a failed attempt at being normal before finally turning his hand to writing. Eventually the voices in his head annoyed him so much that he started writing some of their nonsense down and found that he had a story on his hands. His first book is the forthcoming *Tialoc: Book of Thunder*. He resides in the West Midlands with his wife Samantha and their cat, Oscar.

Bob Veon is an artist from East Palestine, Ohio. His artwork and illustrations have appeared in numerous publications such as *Surprising Stories*, *Whispers of Wickedness*, Jason J.R. Gaskell's *Darkling Light*, *Phobia* and several ebook covers for novellas by Lawrence Dagstine. He is currently working on a LOT of illustration for Lawrence Dagstine's forthcoming collection *From the Depths*. Feel free to come visit him at his website **bobveon.webs.com**.

Nick Walters lives and writes in Bristol. He is the author of several Doctor Who novels including the DWM award-winning *Reckless Engineering*. He is currently working on *Mutually Assured Domination*, a novel in the new *Lethbridge-Stewart* series published by Candy Jar Press.

Made in the USA
Charleston, SC
22 May 2016